the PALOMINO ☆PONY STEALS THE SHOW

Look out for:

the
PALOMINO
✿PONY
COMES
HOME

the
PALOMINO
✿PONY
RIDES
OUT

the
PALOMINO
✿PONY
WINS
THROUGH

the
PALOMINO
✿PONY
RUNS
FREE

the
PALOMINO
✿PONY
ON PARADE

the PaLOMiNO ☆PONY STEALS THE SHOW

OLIVIA TUFFIN

nosy crow

With special thanks to Michelle Misra

First published 2016 by Nosy Crow Ltd
The Crow's Nest, 10a Lant Street
London SE1 1QR
www.nosycrow.com

ISBN: 978 0 85763 628 7

A CIP catalogue record for this book is available from the British Library.

Printed and bound in the UK by Clays Ltd, St Ives Plc.
Typeset by Tiger Media, Bishops Stortford, Hertfordshire

Papers used by Nosy Crow are made from wood grown in
sustainable forests.

1 3 5 7 9 8 6 4 2

To Tammy, thank you for
always believing in Georgia and Lily.

PROLOGUE

The girl gripped the magazine, feeling her jealousy and resentment grow with every word she read. Yet another win for the black pony and his talented jockey. It seemed he was destined for the very top, and so was his rider. Tearing the page into pieces, she scattered them in the breeze as her ponies watched on with interest. The girl stalked up and down the yard in a foul mood. She was surrounded by luxury and wealth, but she was still missing that extra-special something. The black pony had been meant for her. *She* had been the one destined to ride him to glory and she could never forget that.

Angrily kicking the gravel, she drew herself up tall. Next week, that's when it would all change. That's when she would show everyone what she was capable of. She scowled as she furiously sent a text message, knowing it wouldn't bring a reply. But next week the black pony and his rider would realise that she was going to get to the top, and she didn't care how she did it.

CHAPTER ONE

Georgia slowed down as she neared the village post office. "Am I really doing the right thing?" she muttered under her breath.

Twisting the envelope over in her hands, she considered turning away without posting it. But she couldn't do that to Melanie. Not after seeing how happy Melanie had been when she'd received the phone call to tell her that Georgia had been selected for the dressage training camp. Georgia hadn't even known that Janey, head of the Round Barrow Pony Club, had put her name forward. Georgia had said once or twice that she'd like to try something different with her pony, Lily, but she hadn't thought anything more of it!

Now, standing in front of the postbox in the chilly February air, Georgia wavered for another second. Then, taking a deep breath, she slipped the neatly addressed envelope through the slot. She crossed her fingers. This was it – a new adventure for her and Lily. And she knew that she needed to grasp the opportunity with both hands.

☆ ☆ ☆

A couple of hours later, after spending some time with Lily, Georgia walked up the driveway to Dan's farm. Dan Coleman was one of Georgia's best friends.

"Hey, G!" Dan called across to her. He was

4

tinkering with an old piece of machinery in the sunshine, his sandy hair windswept, a streak of oil across his cheek.

It was hard to believe that just two months ago the village of Redgrove had suffered the worst snowstorms in memory. Georgia had ridden through the whiteout on Christmas Eve to stop Dan's father's sheep from being stolen. Now, with the weak winter sun pouring into the yard, and the early snowdrops and daffodils just starting to make an appearance in the beds outside the farm shop, it felt as though the freezing winter was finally on its way out. It wouldn't be long until Georgia and her friends would be able to hack out after school and attend early-summer shows!

"So, did you post it?" Dan asked, wiping the grease off his fingers with an old rag and leaning up against the fence.

Georgia crouched down to say hello to the lambs grazing next to their mothers in the sunshine. "I certainly did," she said with a nod, before grimacing. "There's no going back now."

Dan chuckled. "That's good," he said cheerfully. "And it's only for a week, remember. Although ... I will miss you."

Georgia couldn't help but smile at this. Not only was the snow a distant memory, but so was the memory of the actress Joss McCall-Jones trying to cause trouble between Dan and Georgia. Joss had been starring in a film shot near Redgrove and Lily had made a guest appearance. Joss had fallen for Dan and tried to push Georgia out of the way. But now she was back in London with a new boyfriend and later in the year Dan and Georgia would go to the premiere of the film!

Although she and Dan were mostly back on track, Georgia was still a little unsure of where she stood in the relationship – and whether they were just good friends or something more. Dan had appeared briefly in the film with Lily and Joss and after that his popularity had rocketed at school. He was always being invited to parties or to hang out with classmates, whereas Georgia, completely absorbed in her ponies, was often overlooked. It was slightly unsettling.

"I'll miss you too," she said shyly. "What are you going to do while I'm away?"

"Hmm, just stuff," Dan said casually. "Might see some friends from school, that sort of thing."

"OK." Georgia shrugged, feeling even more unsure. After their recent rocky patch it would have been good to be around for the week they had off school, but the timing couldn't be helped. Dan knew how important the ponies were to Georgia. And it was only a week.

Lily and Georgia were going to be put through

their paces by the country's leading trainers! And at the end of the week, one of the riders would be taken forward to funded training and the chance to ride in the Young Riders Pony Squad. Despite Georgia's earlier reservations, she was starting to look forward to the camp. She just hoped she could live up to Janey and Melanie's expectations!

✩ ✩ ✩

"You won't forget about me, will you?" Emma, Georgia's best friend, looked her straight in the eye as the two girls lounged on the sofa in Emma's parents' house later that evening, sharing a bowl of crisps and flicking through the television channels.

"Emma!" Playfully, Georgia prodded her friend's arm. Emma grinned in reply.

"Oh, come on, Georgia," Emma continued. "You're bound to get picked for training."

"Hmm," Georgia said, a frown creasing her forehead. "I don't know about that. Anyway, sponsorship didn't exactly work out for Jasper, did it?" she said, referring to Janey's assistant instructor. Jasper had been a former top junior show rider and was the older brother of Will Bowen. Will's pony, Santa, was a livery at Redgrove.

"No," Emma agreed, reaching across Georgia for another handful of crisps. "But this training will be properly funded."

The two teenagers sat in silence for a while as Georgia tried to comprehend this. Her little palomino pony had become a famous name in the showing world, and had been the subject of many glowing reports in the national horsey press, but could they progress further and take on dressage? It would be interesting to see how the training week panned out. Drawing her knees up to her chest Georgia hugged them close, feeling equally excited and terrified.

"So what's going on with you, Em?" Georgia asked finally.

"Oh, the usual," Emma giggled. "And … I'm going on a date with Will during half-term."

"No way!" Georgia nudged her friend. "That's brilliant!"

Emma grinned. "You'll need to give me some help planning what to wear!"

"Er … not sure I'll be much help in that department." Georgia smiled. "I knew there was a reason you'd been helping out at Redgrove more!"

"You got me, G." Emma grinned again.

Georgia was pleased for her friend, and felt a tiny pang of envy about life carrying on as usual at Redgrove while she and Lily were away. Then, remembering how she had felt before her work experience on the Smalley show yard, she gave herself a mental shake. Redgrove would be just the same when she got back, and she was off on a new adventure!

CHAPTER TWO

Georgia wasn't feeling quite so confident a few days later as she tried to shut her suitcase, which was overflowing with her riding kit, chaps, gloves and jodhpurs. "Oh, come on," she muttered to herself as she sat down on the top of her case. All the paperwork relating to the camp was sitting neatly on her bedside table, ready to take to Redgrove Farm in the morning. Melanie was going to be driving her and Lily to the prestigious yard deep in the Cotswolds.

Emma and Georgia had spent an evening researching the equestrian centre on the computer. Georgia had been blown away by the photographs showing a beautiful honey-coloured stone-built stable block set in the grounds of a huge manor house, flanked with neatly striped lawns. There was even an Olympic-sized indoor arena, and an outdoor arena built within a walled garden, roses trailing over the warm bricks.

As well as regular competitions and events, and stabling liveries for some of the richest clients in the county, Rosefolly Equestrian Centre was used as a training base for some of the country's leading riders. Rifling through her wardrobe when she had got home from Emma's, Georgia had pulled out her faithful old navy jodhs and gazed at them for a few minutes, before catching a bus to the saddler's shop the very next day and buying the checked breeches she had always coveted.

"All OK, sweetheart?" Hearing her mum's voice, Georgia looked up and saw the door being nudged open by a black-and-white muzzle. Her spaniel, Pip, bounded joyfully into her room, closely followed by her mum, who sat down on Georgia's bed, her hands curled round a cup of tea. "It'll be quiet without you."

"I know," Georgia said with a smile, doing up the zip on her suitcase and pausing to stroke Pip. "But I'll be back before you know it."

Picking up a photo of Lily, her mum gazed at it for a minute. "She really has opened doors for you, hasn't she?" she said, the pride in her voice unmistakable.

Georgia smiled. Her mum was just as proud of Lily's achievements in the show ring as Georgia was. Georgia often wondered what she would be doing if she hadn't found Lily on her school trip. She was pretty sure she would still be helping at Redgrove, grooming Callie, and riding Wilson when Sophie wasn't around, but Mum was right – Lily coming into her life had opened up a whole new world of opportunity, and the week ahead was proof of that. But just how far did Georgia *want* to go with Lily? She needed to find that out for herself.

☆ ☆ ☆

Redgrove had never looked prettier as Georgia's mum drove up the gravelled drive early the next morning. A wisp of smoke was winding its way up from the chimney. *Melanie must have her log burner going*, Georgia thought, picturing the terriers curled up in front of it and Simon, Melanie's husband, frying eggs on the hob. She felt a wave of homesickness already, thinking of Pip, who had been left curled up in her basket. But at least Georgia would be with Lily for the week!

The lights were on in the stables, casting a warm glow over the cobbles, and Will, wrapped up warm in a blue-and-white striped scarf, gave her a cheerful wave as she clambered out of the car. He was pushing the wheelbarrow towards the stable where his pony, Santa, was enjoying a mouthful of hay. The four ponies looked settled and content as they stuck their heads over the stable doors.

Lily whickered a greeting as Georgia lifted her suitcase out of the back of the car and set it down next to her stable. Lily's trunk was all ready to go. It held her saddle and bridle, grooming kit and boots, plus a box of little extras that Melanie had sorted out – things like a first-aid kit and spare reins. They were all set to go, and Georgia took a deep breath as she hugged her mum goodbye, just as Melanie emerged from the house.

16

"All set, G?" Melanie smiled at Georgia.

"As ready as I'll ever be," she said, giving her mum one final hug.

Will appeared by her side, carrying Santa's head collar. "Do you know anyone going?" he asked cheerfully.

Georgia shook her head, reaching into her backpack for the training-camp information. "No," she said, handing it to him. "Do you recognise any of the names?"

Scanning the letter, Will squinted at the list of attendees. "I don't think so," he said, shaking his head. "Well, I kind of know the names, but remember, it's a whole different world to the show ring. They must all be dressage riders."

Georgia heard her name being called and, glancing up, saw Melanie pulling down the lorry ramp. She needed to quickly boot Lily up for the journey to Rosefolly and put her belongings into the cab.

Will turned back to his morning chores. "Good luck, G!" he called encouragingly. "Just text me if you need to."

Then all thoughts of any riders on the course were forgotten as Georgia's heart leapt at the sight of Dan rushing through the gates into the yard, slightly out of breath, his cheeks pink with exertion. From the mud splattered up the back of his jeans, it looked as though he had run all the way over from his farm to the yard. Georgia led Lily out of her stable; she was wearing her travelling kit and looked a million dollars. Dan reached up and patted her golden neck. "Good luck, girl," he said with a grin, and then shyly enveloped Georgia in a hug. "And good luck, G," he whispered into her hair, slightly awkwardly.

"Thanks," Georgia muttered, blushing as she noticed Will giving her a thumbs-up sign

behind Dan's back.

"Text me any time," Dan said, echoing Will. "If it gets too much, I'll come and rescue you!"

"What? On your tractor?" Georgia laughed self-consciously, and Dan winked.

Then it was time for Georgia to load Lily. As she walked the little mare out of the yard, she heard Dan planning a game of football with Will in the bottom meadow. Glancing behind her at Wilson, Callie and Santa and the terriers chasing each other round the cobbled yard, Georgia took a deep breath as she led Lily quietly up the ramp of the horsebox. She knew she was only going for a week, so why did this feel like the end of an era?

☆ ☆ ☆

Melanie and Georgia chatted easily during the journey to Rosefolly. After they had stopped at a motorway service station to check Lily was OK, and for Melanie to grab a coffee, Georgia thought

19

again about the other riders taking part in the week alongside her. Digging around in her bag, she pulled out the forms again. "Do you know any of the riders going?" she asked Melanie once she had pulled safely out on to the motorway and settled back into the driving.

Mel frowned. "Not sure," she said. "Read them to me and I'll see if I recognise any names."

"OK," Georgia said and, reading aloud, she recited from the list. "Sebastian Woodley, Jodie Harrison, Ellie Baker, Serena Van der Hawk..."

"What was that?" Melanie looked thoughtful.

"Serena Van der Hawk," Georgia repeated slowly. "She sounds very posh!"

Melanie screwed up her forehead. "Serena... Serena..." she muttered, and then clicked her fingers in recognition. "I've got it!" she said triumphantly. "Van der Hawk, daughter of Michael."

Georgia looked blank, and Mel chuckled. "Sorry,

G, probably a bit before your time," she said kindly. "Michael Van der Hawk was a top rider a few years ago, actually before you were even born. Serena is about your age, I'd guess. She will have some lovely ponies; they are very into their horses, although Michael was a bit of a shady character, if I remember. I wonder if Serena can replicate her father's success – he went to a fair few championships, if I recall. Very talented."

Georgia nodded, still no clearer. It would be exciting to meet the daughter of a famous rider though; Georgia was always looking to learn new things about horses, and maybe Serena would be a new friend.

Gazing out of the window at the frost clinging to the hedgerows, Georgia felt a shiver of excitement as the lorry neared Rosefolly. What could be better – a week full of ponies and nothing else!

CHAPTER THREE

Georgia gaped at the surroundings as the big green lorry drove towards the equestrian centre. The drive seemed to go on for miles, winding through expansive parkland with a lake shimmering through the bare trees.

"Look," Melanie chuckled, clearly amused as a peacock wandered nonchalantly in front of them as they pulled into the yard. "You wouldn't find

one of those at Redgrove!"

"Redgrove's better though," Georgia said loyally. "With or without a peacock!"

"Well, it's home to me and I love it." Melanie smiled, and then she paused, looking around. "You know, Lily's got a real future, if you want it." She gazed out at the huge yard. "I'm happy to train you and take you to shows ... but perhaps you could go even further with some real expertise."

Georgia looked at Melanie in surprise. It was the first time she had ever said anything like that. She knew Melanie loved the little palomino just as much as she did, and Georgia, in turn, respected and looked up to Melanie. Her face must have registered her thoughts because Melanie smiled kindly. "I don't think either of us would have thought we were rescuing an Olympia champion that day in Wales, would we?" she chuckled. "I'm just saying there's only so far I can take you, if you want to aim higher. This is your chance to shine, Georgia. Take this opportunity, and grab it and run. Lily's too good not to go further."

The two sat in silence for a minute as Georgia reflected on what Melanie had said. Then Melanie smiled broadly, unbuckled her seat belt and patted Georgia on the shoulder. "Come on!" she said cheerfully, jumping down from the cab. "Let's get Lily settled in."

Lily was used to staying away from Redgrove and was relaxed anywhere – as long as Georgia was there. Soon she was happily munching from a hay net in a huge stable. Georgia and Melanie went to look around. The whole yard was beautiful, and the livery horses looked happy and content, with every need catered for. A young groom had shown them where to go, and had left them to settle in. Georgia was going to meet the rest of the students later, in the barn on the opposite side of the courtyard that doubled up as the meeting room and dining room. Georgia's suitcase was already in her dorm room; the girls were staying in the eaves above the stable block. Georgia had taken ages to walk up the stairs to her living quarters, fascinated by the endless photos of horses adorning the walls and the rich horsey heritage that surrounded Rosefolly. Now, putting her arms round Lily, she felt slightly more confident. They had been hand-selected to take part in the week, and that had to count for something, surely!

"Time for me to say goodbye," Melanie said, rubbing the white stripe running down the centre of Lily's golden face. The little mare closed her eyes happily. Then, turning to Georgia, she patted her shoulder. "And good luck, G," she said warmly. "I'm so proud of you both."

Left alone with Lily, Georgia rolled up her sleeves to look at her watch. It was only two o'clock and she wasn't meeting the other students in the barn until three. Just enough time to give Lily a groom.

Picking up her body brush, she set to work on Lily's golden coat, which was just starting to show a hint of summer dapple through her full clip. Chatting away to her pony, who flicked her ears back and forth as if listening, Georgia was so engrossed in her grooming routine that she almost didn't hear the softly spoken "hello" over her stable door. Turning round, she jumped as she noticed a girl about her age standing outside her stable, holding a leather head collar.

"Hello!" Georgia said brightly.

The girl gave a shy smile. "I'm Jodie," she said, giving a little wave. "And this must be Lily, I've read loads about her in the pony mags."

"That's right!" Georgia grinned, giving Lily a pat. It still amazed her when people recognised the little mare but she had featured in all the horsey publications recently, following her Olympia win. And she was extremely striking with her golden coat.

"I'm next door to you," Jodie continued, gesturing to the stable adjacent to Lily where a black pony's head popped over, mouth full of hay and eyes bright. Jodie smiled and reached across to stroke the pony's delicate muzzle. As small as Lily, who stood just under thirteen hands, but finer, Jodie's pony was a gelding. He wasn't native, Georgia was sure about that, but he looked like a show pony, or a miniature thoroughbred.

"Wow," Georgia breathed, always appreciative of a gorgeous-looking pony, and guessing Jodie's family must be seriously horsey and wealthy to have such a beautiful pony. "He's amazing!"

Jodie looked proud and smiled. "Thanks! He's called Jackson. He's my pride and joy. Hey, shall we go to the barn together for the intro talk?"

"Sure!" Georgia said, pleased. Jodie seemed nice and it would be good to have someone to go with. After putting Lily's rug back on, and after Jodie had checked that Jackson had enough hay, the two girls made their way across to the meeting barn, where the other riders were starting to assemble.

There was a tall, thin man inside, wearing a bomber jacket and chaps and talking quietly with a pretty young woman, wearing equally smart riding gear. They both nodded at Georgia and Jodie, gesturing for them to come in. "We'll be with you in a few minutes," the man said, nodding curtly in their direction.

The low buzz of chatter paused as the girls sat down on a squishy sofa covered with a Newmarket blanket, opposite another pair of teenagers. A girl with bright-red hair gave a small wave and the boy next to her unfolded long legs and gave a lazy smile, reaching out his hand in greeting. Georgia shook it, feeling shy.

"I'm Sebastian Woodley," the boy drawled in a refined Home Counties accent. "And this is Ellie," he said, gesturing to the girl with red hair, as she and Jodie introduced themselves. Sebastian turned his attention to her. "So you must be Georgia," he continued, "with the show pony."

Georgia nodded and was just about to reply when a girl with long dark hair, sunglasses and a smart black riding jacket swept in and sat down next to Sebastian. Georgia heard Jodie draw in her breath sharply. "Serena!"

"Hi, Jodie," she sneered. The words were friendly but Serena's voice was icy. Georgia realised immediately that they knew each other. You could cut the tension between them with a knife.

Jodie shrank back into her seat, barely whispering a reply. Sebastian carried on with his introductions.

"Serena, this is Georgia," he said, waving a hand towards her. "The showing girl."

Serena flicked her dark mane over one shoulder. She was as polished and glossy as the dressage horses that filled the luxurious boxes at Rosefolly. "Oh, yes," she said in a flat voice. "I heard you were joining us." She spread her long elegant fingers, examining the manicured nails. "Not being funny, but showing's a bit different to dressage, isn't it? I mean, don't you just ride in a circle?"

Georgia looked at her, slightly taken back by her bluntness.

Sebastian grinned. "Oh, come on, Serena," he said cheerfully. "Georgia won Olympia at Christmas; that's quite a big deal."

"Yes, I'm aware," Serena hissed. "I do read *Horse & Hound* every week." She took off her sunglasses and fixed Georgia with a cold stare. "Rosefolly's training camps are pretty exclusive," she continued. "Be interesting to see how your *Welsh pony* copes." She put extra emphasis on the words 'Welsh pony', as if driving home a point.

Georgia was too startled to think of a reply. She had never met anyone quite as blunt as Serena, and she was surprised that anyone still had that attitude when native ponies up and down the country were doing well in all sorts of disciplines.

With one last glare at Georgia, Serena turned her attention to Sebastian. As the two of them chatted away, it became clear they knew each other from the young riders' circuit. It sounded a world away from Redgrove.

Serena gossiped at length about her recent pony-buying trip to Germany, and Sebastian filled her in on news he had heard from his trainers. They were so glamorous and self-assured, despite seeming to be the same age as Georgia. Georgia suddenly thought of Redgrove and felt a twinge of homesickness. Once again she reminded herself it was only a week, and made a mental note to keep out of Serena's way. At least Sebastian seemed OK, even if Serena was all over him.

The thin man in the bomber jacket at the front of the room clapped his hands, making everyone jump, and the chat quickly died away. "Welcome, everyone," he said in a brusque voice, his piercing eyes boring into each and every attendee. Even Serena was listening quietly. "Some of you – Sebastian and Serena – may know me from past training days here at Rosefolly, but for those of you who don't, I'm Henry Winters, *chief* instructor. This is Daisy. She's new to Rosefolly and she'll be helping me this week."

The young woman next to him smiled warmly, a sharp contrast to Henry's steely expression.

"First things first," Henry started. "Rules. We have very high standards here at Rosefolly and any rule-breaking could see you leaving the course. Please read through your welcome letters."

Glancing down at the letter Georgia had been handed on arrival at the barn, she skim-read the bullet-pointed list of rules. They were mostly standard yard things – stables to be mucked out before eight a.m., riding hats to meet current safety standards, and so on. Georgia noticed no one was allowed on the yard after nine p.m. and felt a twinge of sadness. Lily was so close to her and yet she couldn't even sneak down to kiss her goodnight. Still, glancing at Henry's stern face, she decided there was no way she wanted to break the rules and make him angry!

After running through the week's itinerary, it seemed that the riders were free to go and settle in for the afternoon. Chattering excitedly, they spilled out into the sunny courtyard. Georgia noticed Serena had hung back and was soon deep in conversation with Henry. She might have imagined it, but she could have sworn they looked towards Georgia as they spoke. Shrugging, she caught up with Jodie, who was heading back to the stables to unload the rest of Jackson's kit.

"What was all that about?" Georgia said when she was sure they were out of earshot. "With Serena, I mean. She was really unfriendly with you. And pretty off with me."

Jodie glanced around, her face blank. "Oh," she mumbled. "I'd just keep out of her way if I were you. I certainly will." Georgia looked at her in surprise. "Serena's family and mine – well, they go way back," Jodie explained.

And with that, Jodie turned quickly back to Jackson, burying her head in his neck.

CHAPTER FOUR

"So, tell me all about it."

After a long day it was a relief to chat to Dan on her mobile, as Georgia leaned on the door to Lily's stable, watching the little mare as she quietly ate her supper. Georgia had managed to take Lily for a walk-in-hand to stretch her legs, and allow the palomino to graze. She had settled in really well and was totally at ease in the plush surroundings.

Georgia paused. "It's OK," she said. "There's a nice girl next door to me, but the others, well, they're a bit... Oh, I don't know. It doesn't matter."

"Well, we are all really proud of you." Dan said, not pushing her.

"So what have you been up to today?" Georgia asked once she had told Dan about Rosefolly.

"Just playing football with Will," Dan replied casually. "And I'm just about to help Dad move the cows."

"That's nice," Georgia said. She missed the normality of Redgrove, particularly after meeting Serena. Still, maybe they had just got off on the wrong foot. Once Lily was in the arena, Georgia could show just how capable they were as a pair, and prove Serena wrong. Saying goodbye to Dan, she put her phone back in her pocket, feeling a lot more positive.

the
PALOMINO
✧PONY

✿ ✿ ✿

To Georgia's disappointment, Serena was just as unfriendly the next morning. When the five young riders sat down to have breakfast, she barely even acknowledged Georgia, Jodie or Ellie, but gave Sebastian a kiss on both cheeks, proclaiming her welcome loudly.

Sebastian grinned as he sat down opposite Jodie and Georgia, digging into the bacon and eggs with gusto. Then he looked a little closer at Jodie. "Hey," he said, squinting at her carefully. "Don't I know you from somewhere? I mean, not from shows."

Jodie reddened. "Probably," she muttered.

Serena leaned over and answered for her. "Jodie's mum used to be our groom," she sneered. "So you've probably seen Jodie hanging around. Her mum works at Rosefolly now."

Georgia looked at Jodie in surprise. So *that* was how the families were connected. She had just presumed that with such a beautiful pony, Jodie was from a wealthy competition family, like Serena.

"So, how's Jackson?" Serena continued, her voice cold.

"He's fine," Jodie mumbled, looking down at her untouched breakfast.

"Amazed he got through to this week." Serena laughed unkindly. "Horrid pony. Completely talentless and impossible to ride." Even Sebastian looked embarrassed as Serena glared at Jodie. "I mean, who would want a pony like that?"

Georgia, unable to listen to any more, stopped her. "What *is* your problem?" she said hotly. Serena was obviously a bully and poor Jodie was her target.

"My problem?" Serena chuckled, gathering up her belongings. "You should ask her what *her* problem is. And don't get involved," she hissed, shooting Georgia a dark look. "Come on, Seb. I'm

going to the stables."

With that, the two teenagers sauntered off, but not before Sebastian had shot Jodie a sympathetic grin.

Once they had left the building Georgia turned to Jodie, who had left her breakfast untouched. "Can you believe that?" Georgia cried. "She's so rude! Why is she so horrible about your pony?"

Jumping up, Jodie grabbed her riding hat and pushed her chair back with a screech. "I don't need you fighting my battles," she muttered, her eyes ablaze. "Just leave it!"

And with that, she ran off towards the stables. Awkwardly, Georgia followed her. She tacked Lily up in total silence, and Jodie did the same in the neighbouring stable. She longed to chat to her new friend but Jodie was completely avoiding eye contact. A friendly-looking woman pushing a wheelbarrow paused next to Jackson's stable and spoke in a low voice to Jodie. Georgia couldn't hear what was said but from the way the lady pushed Jodie's hair behind her ears and patted her shoulder, Georgia guessed that it must be Jodie's mum. She was tall and looked kind, wearing faded jeans and a wax jacket, which reminded Georgia a little bit of Melanie. Jodie's mum turned to Georgia, smiling.

"So this must be Lily," she said, in the same soft voice as Jodie's. "We've all been so excited to have the Olympia champion here at Rosefolly. It's a shame the yard owners are away – they would have loved to have met her. I hear she's causing quite a stir on the show circuit!"

Georgia blushed with pleasure. Jodie's mum seemed really nice and it was a change to have someone friendly to talk to. But before she could reply, she looked up to see Henry Winters striding across the yard.

"Amanda," he barked as he neared Jodie's mum.

Lily, used to Redgrove where no one ever raised their voice, flung her head up in alarm and Georgia put her arms round her.

Henry didn't look happy. "I told you that Lady Harris was visiting her horse today, and he's filthy, with stable stains all over his side. It's just not good enough."

Amanda, Jodie's mum, turned to Henry. "I'm so sorry. He had a bath this morning in the hot wash, but he must have rolled in the stable."

"Well, sort it out," Henry said coldly. "Now."

Without another word, Amanda went off to sort the livery horse. Henry turned on his heel and headed towards the outdoor arena, completely ignoring both girls. He was totally awful, Georgia thought, and turned to Jodie, who was leaning on Jackson's glossy black neck and looking upset.

"You OK?" Georgia whispered, forgetting

41

Jodie's earlier outburst.

Jodie nodded miserably. "Yeah," she said. "Henry's just got it in for Mum, like usual. She's the head groom here, and he's always really hard on her."

Georgia looked at her in surprise. She hadn't even been at Rosefolly for a day but she could tell the head groom did a great job – the yard was immaculate, and happy, healthy horses filled the clean and airy stables. It had only been a stable stain, and all horses got them when they lay down. "What's his problem?" Georgia asked curiously.

"Just yard stuff," Jodie mumbled, turning back to Jackson and adjusting his bridle. "The owners of Rosefolly, Martha and James, are really nice and they love Mum. But they are in Australia visiting family, and Henry's been left in charge. For some reason he keeps having a go at Mum." She lowered her voice, glancing around to check no one was listening. "If you ask me," she whispered, "he's letting the power go to his head." Then, giving Jackson a pat, she opened her stable door. "Come on. Henry hates late students. We don't want a black mark on the first day."

CHAPTER FIVE

As she warmed up in the vast walled arena, Georgia almost had to pinch herself. All of her horsey heroes had ridden here at some point and now here she was, trotting round on the little palomino pony. Lily was feeling great, and stretched her neck forward as Georgia gave her her head, letting her work long and low, relaxing into her stride. It gave her a chance to assess the other riders while Henry Winters leaned against the fence, talking to the friendlier instructor, Daisy.

Sebastian's pony was seriously gorgeous. About fourteen hands, he had rippling muscles and a glossy bay coat, while white bandages on all four legs gave an air of professionalism. Serena was working-in at the far end of the arena. Like Sebastian's bay, the pony Serena was riding looked like a mini warmblood. A rich liver chestnut with four white socks and a noble white face, the pony was performing a beautiful shoulder-in as Serena sat unmoving in the saddle. Ellie's pony was a pretty grey mare.

Alongside Jackson, the other four ponies were highly bred, and Georgia couldn't help but notice that Lily was the only native type. She was also the only one not wearing white bandages or a sparkly brow band. Even Jodie had put snow-white bandages on Jackson's slim legs, and the crystals on his bridle shimmered and glinted in the winter sunshine. Lily was wearing her show saddle with the plain brown numnah underneath, and her bridle was simple Havana leather. Georgia was glad she had her new checked breeches on, but still felt very plain next to the other four students. Will had been right – dressage was definitely different to showing!

Georgia watched the other students closely. To her surprise, Serena wasn't as elegant in the saddle as she had first appeared. Sure, she was in the correct position and her pony was turned out beautifully, but the whole picture was slightly wrong somehow. Thinking about it, Georgia was reminded of Jemma, Lily's previous rider. Technically excellent, but totally unsympathetic. Georgia turned her attention to Sebastian. He was a lovely rider, his long legs hanging still and quiet as his pony cantered a perfect twenty-metre circle.

It was the same with Ellie, the red-haired girl Georgia had met the night before. Georgia looked forward to learning what she could from her fellow riders! And then there was Jodie. Georgia had had the opportunity to watch some amazing riders – but Jodie was in another league. Watching with pleasure, Georgia noticed her feather-light hands and the subtlest of aids she used to encourage Jackson to dance across the arena. With Jodie's long ponytail bouncing in time to the shiny black pony's rhythm, the pair were mesmerising.

Georgia watched Daisy smile with pleasure as she leaned on the fence watching Jackson pass. Henry's face, however, was as unsmiling and cold as usual, speaking only to Serena as she trotted past him.

The group assembled in the centre of the arena once everyone had sufficiently warmed up, where they were joined by Henry and Daisy. They were each to ride a five-minute simple dressage test, called out by Daisy as Henry watched. Sebastian was up first and rode a lovely test, perfectly striking off into a balanced canter, his bay pony's mane flying.

"Super!" Daisy beamed.

Henry nodded. "Not bad, could be better," he said gruffly. "Watch those hands."

Sebastian shrugged and joined his place in the line-up. Ellie's test was as equally pleasing to watch, but Henry was still full of criticism. Ellie's sunny face dropped as he pulled apart her position and her pony's stride. She rode meekly back into line, and Georgia wondered how Henry could have rubbished her riding so much, when she had been really very good.

Georgia was next. Lily trotted beautifully up the centre line as Georgia listened carefully for her next instruction, and she managed a good test. It wasn't all that different to her showing performance really, and Lily's floating trot and light canter soon had Daisy beaming again.

"Lovely!" she enthused. "You're the first native pony that I've taught here at Rosefolly, and what a pony!"

Georgia, patting Lily, rode her back into line on a long rein, her legs trembling. Phew, Lily had proved her right to be here.

Sebastian looked impressed, as did Ellie and Jodie, who gave her a thumbs-up. Only Serena sat looking stonily ahead, her eyes cold. Georgia almost felt like sticking her tongue out as if to say, *"See what my Welsh pony can do!"*

"Well, I'm certainly looking forward to the next few days," Daisy continued happily. "Just watch your transitions, Georgia. We can work on sharpening them up. What do you think, Henry?" She turned to the tall instructor, who was moodily adjusting the collar on his jacket.

"OK," he said flatly, barely looking up. "Mare's not got much more to give though, not when compared to a sports pony. It's just not got the scope."

Georgia felt as though someone had poured cold water on her, as Daisy frowned at her colleague.

"That's not fair," she said firmly. "I thought that was excellent."

"Oh well, you're new, you'll learn." Henry was inspecting his fingernails now, completely uninterested. "We will see. Serena!"

As Henry called her name, Serena rode forward, giving Georgia a triumphant look, as if to say, *"I told you so."*

Her cheeks burning, Georgia watched as Serena ran through the test. After Sebastian's and Ellie's riding, Serena just didn't match up. The lovely pony she was riding was an obvious schoolmaster but there was no partnership between the two. Coming down the centre line, the pony's handsome chestnut head started snaking, frustrated at being held on such a tight rein. Georgia noticed Daisy grimace slightly and then look startled as Henry praised Serena in a booming voice. "Now, that," he said triumphantly, "is how you do it."

Even Sebastian looked confused.

Serena smiled, a cool, tight smile as she took her place back in the line-up, not bothering to pat her pony. Jodie's face was blank as she nudged Jackson towards the instructors, where Daisy greeted her with a smile but Henry barely glanced at her.

The contrast between Jodie's and Serena's riding was clear to see. Jackson was obviously a tricky, hot pony but Jodie sat so quietly and so softly in the saddle that all his energy was concentrated on a perfect extended trot and an uphill bouncing canter. He looked as though he was on the cusp of exploding the whole time but somehow Jodie rode him beautifully and Georgia was entranced.

Daisy clearly felt the same as she was full of praise for the young student. She turned to Henry, clearly expecting that he must feel the same.

But if Henry had been critical of Georgia, poor Jodie was torn to shreds. Georgia could only pick up snatches of the conversation, but heard enough to know Henry was being unnecessarily nasty.

Poor Jodie rode back to the line-up, her eyes brimming with unspilled tears, causing Serena to smirk even more.

Once the assessment was over, the rest of the lesson fared no better and despite Daisy's protests, Jodie and Jackson were picked on mercilessly. Georgia didn't do much better. Although she felt that she was riding really well, and the arena mirrors showed a pony and rider in perfect harmony, Henry barked at her the whole time.

The only rider he praised was Serena, and again, Georgia couldn't work out why. She was far from perfect.

Ending the lesson, Henry turned on his heel and stalked off. Daisy was waiting for Jodie and Georgia as they exited the vast arena. Patting Jackson and Lily, she tried to cheer the teenagers up.

"You both did beautifully," she said kindly, obviously confused by Henry's attitude.

But despite Daisy's words of encouragement, Georgia felt her legs tremble as she untacked Lily and put on her wool rug. She leaned against the little palomino's solid side, the pony's warmth giving Georgia comfort. She had decided there and then that she hated Henry, not just because of the way he had picked on her new friend Jodie, but because of the way he had referred to Lily as "it"!

Chapter Six

Curled up later, wrapped in a dressing gown after a warm bath, Georgia felt slightly better. She'd had a lesson in the afternoon with Daisy when, guided by her gentle but expert tuition, she and Lily had perfected the shoulder-in down the long side of the arena. Even so, she couldn't keep the wobble out of her voice as she picked up the phone to Dan that evening. He'd told her to ring him every day, and she was going to, needing a bit of normality.

"Hey, G!" Dan sounded as cheerful as ever.

Just hearing his friendly voice, Georgia felt her bottom lip start to tremble and she took a deep breath. She clearly needed to grow a thicker skin if she was going to survive in the equestrian world. "Hey," she said as brightly as possible.

Dan picked up on her emotion straight away. "What's up, Georgia?" he asked, sounding concerned.

"Oh," Georgia sniffed. "It sounds stupid but the instructor's a real bully. I've made a friend but there's something weird going on here, and to top it off there's a girl who hates me for no reason."

"Come on, G!" Dan said positively. "It's only for a week. Just ride like you always do, and ignore the bullies."

Just hearing Dan's voice cheered Georgia up and she wiped her eyes. He was right; her riding should speak for itself. Janey wouldn't have chosen her to go forward if she didn't believe in her. Changing the subject, Georgia's voice brightened as she asked Dan what he had been doing that day.

"Farm stuff, and playing football with Will," Dan said vaguely, after the briefest of pauses.

"Again?" Georgia sounded surprised, although she didn't mean to. It was just that Dan wasn't really a football fan.

"Well, I've got to do something when you're not around!" Dan chuckled. "Speak tomorrow, G, and remember, we're all here for you."

☆ ☆ ☆

Georgia took her place beside Jodie in the common room after supper, while Jodie waited for her mum to finish her shift. The room was horsey heaven – stacks of *Horse & Hound* to read, and a whole wall of rosettes. Inspired by the photos and horsey history surrounding them, Georgia and Jodie were soon deep in conversation about their ponies. Picking up a framed photo of a rider at a dressage world championship, Jodie gazed at it. "That's what I want," she said quietly.

"To be famous?" Georgia asked curiously, and Jodie shook her head.

"Not necessarily famous," she explained. "I just want to be the best. I want to get as far as I can. Jackson's capable."

Her voice was determined, and Georgia nodded. "I believe you," she said.

"I just don't want Mum to struggle," Jodie continued, gazing back down at the photograph. "Jackson ... he's my one chance."

Feeling as though she and Jodie could talk to each other now, and glad that she had at least one friend at Rosefolly, Georgia decided to broach the subject of Serena and Jackson. She was curious as to how Jodie came to have such a fantastic but quirky pony – a pony that Serena obviously knew, but hated for some reason.

Dropping her voice slightly, Jodie started to speak. "Serena's dad purchased Jackson for a huge amount of money in Germany," she said. "He was supposed to be Serena's star ride. Jackson may be talented but he's also a tricky character and *very* sensitive. Serena wanted results immediately and, well, she clashed pretty much straight away with him."

"I knew someone like that," Georgia grimacing, and Jodie nodded.

"Lily's old owner?" she asked. "I followed what happened. You've done so well with Lily."

"So how did you end up with Jackson?" Georgia continued, hooked on Jodie's story.

"I used to go up with Mum when I wasn't at school," said Jodie. "Serena and I were quite friendly back then." Jodie pushed her thick hair out of her eyes. "Mum kept her horse at Serena's yard – he was the most amazing warmblood and she was doing really well on him, winning loads of shows and dressage competitions. It was then I started to notice that Serena and Jackson weren't getting along. Mum told me that Serena's dad was going to have him put down because he was dangerous." She paused, before continuing. "I was really upset, and begged her dad to let me try Jackson, the day before he was due to go." She smiled at the memory. "Well, we got on straight away. I don't know why, but we just clicked."

"That's obvious," Georgia agreed, thinking back to their lessons today. "You ride him so well! So what's Serena's problem?"

Jodie shrugged, again looking around to check no one was listening. "Jealousy, I think," she whispered. "She's never got over the fact that *she* couldn't ride Jackson. And when we started doing well, she just got worse."

Georgia absorbed this for a couple of moments. "So your mum bought him?" she asked carefully, and Jodie's face clouded over.

"Yes," she said, looking upset. "But she sold her horse to Serena's dad in exchange. He was going to keep him for her so she could still have the ride, as she still worked for him. But he sold him to Germany for five times what he paid Mum just a few months later, and Mum walked out of her job after that. She was heartbroken." She turned to look at Georgia, her eyes ablaze with determination. "Don't you see?" she said fiercely. "I've got to succeed, for Mum, and everything she gave up! Jackson's won everything I've ever entered, but I can't do it on my own. That's why I'm here. I really want this, Georgia."

Georgia was humbled into silence. Jodie wasn't just after rosettes and glory; she really wanted to ride to the top. It meant everything to her.

"But what about you?" Jodie said, changing the subject. "What do you want to achieve?"

Georgia thought hard about what Jodie had just said. It made her realise with a start that really she had already achieved her dream – having her own pony, or as close as possible as she would get for a while. She smiled at her new friend. "I just wanted my own pony," she shrugged. "That was my dream, and now it's come true. I have Lily."

"That was my dream!"

A mocking laugh made both Georgia and Jodie jump, as Serena appeared from nowhere behind them accompanied by Sebastian, who had the collar of his shirt turned up and a lazy grin on his face. "My name's Georgia and I'm totally pony *mwad!*" Serena continued in a mocking baby voice, as Georgia's cheeks burned with mortification. She looked at Sebastian, hoping he wasn't joining in, but to her disappointment he was laughing alongside Serena. So much for him being OK!

Jodie was silent, looking down at her feet.

"Pur-lease," Serena continued, her flat mocking tone full of scorn. "You do know where you are, don't you? You're at Rosefolly, the best equestrian centre in the country. This isn't little farm-pony stuff, and as for you, Jodie, goodness knows how that mad pony got here. He's downright dangerous."

Georgia could take no more. "Oh yeah?" she shot back, her cheeks burning but feeling brave. "At least Jodie can ride Jackson, unlike you!"

The laughter died on Serena's lips. "What have you said?" she hissed at Jodie, her eyes ablaze.

"Nothing," Jodie mumbled. "I just told her that Mum bought Jackson from you, that's all."

"You'd better watch yourself, Jodie Harrison," Serena said threateningly. "I thought I'd made it clear before we came." She looked straight at Jodie, her voice icy. "While Henry's in charge, your mum might want to watch her back. You'd be really stuck if she lost her poxy little job."

CHAPTER SEVEN

"Come on, Jodie, she's just talking nonsense," Georgia tried to reassure her friend later that evening. They had escaped down to the stables together to hang out with the ponies, and were sitting on the hay bales in the alleyway across from the ponies' boxes, eating the chocolate biscuits they had sneaked out of the canteen. "Serena can't really get your mum fired; she's just being stupid."

Jodie shook her head miserably. She was wrapped in Jackson's navy wool rug. "No," she said quietly. "But you've seen the way Henry favours her. She texted me before we came, warning me off, but I didn't believe it. That's why I was trying to keep out of her way."

Georgia nodded, listening. Henry was obviously an expert rider and instructor, so why was he praising Serena's riding and yet pulling apart Jodie, who in Georgia's opinion was the best rider on the course? "Hopefully he will see sense soon," she said firmly.

A bleep from her pocket broke the silence that followed, and pulling her phone out she couldn't help a smile escape her lips when she saw it was Dan.

"Hey, G!"

Georgia could practically hear his cheerful voice as she read the text:

Hope it's gone well today. Call me later. x

Georgia sent a quick reply to let him know how things were, as well as asking him what he had been doing that day.

Football with Will. x

The reply came back as quick as a flash, much to Georgia's bemusement. That was surely the third day in a row that Dan had played football with Will. Something weird was going on.

"Who's that?" Jodie said curiously, noticing Georgia's smile lifting the corners of her mouth.

"My friend Dan," Georgia mumbled.

"Friend?" Jodie grinned, one eyebrow lifting, and Georgia blushed. It was good to forget Serena's threats as they chatted easily about Dan and how much Georgia liked him. Jodie admitted she had a bit of a crush on Sebastian. Georgia could see why – he was handsome and an excellent rider. "It's a shame though," Jodie said miserably, "that he's too wrapped up in Serena to see what she's really like."

"Well, let's hope he sees sense then, as well as Henry," Georgia agreed. "Come on, let's go and check on the ponies."

After the ups and downs of the day, it was a relief to spend some precious time with Lily before the yard curfew. Jodie wasn't staying in the dorms, as her mum lived nearby, and so she left for the evening. Georgia had learned that Jackson wasn't usually stabled at Rosefolly, but at a farm DIY livery yard down the road.

Finding herself alone, but not keen on joining Sebastian and Serena in the common room, she decided to sit and read her book in the vast stone manger in Lily's stable. Ellie was also staying at Rosefolly but she tended to keep to herself in the evenings.

There was something quite comforting about watching the little palomino pull at her hay net, the occasional whicker or snort from horses in the surrounding boxes the only sound. Thinking back to her conversation with Jodie in the common room, Georgia reflected on her friend's words. Jodie really wanted to succeed as a top rider, which Georgia totally understood. But the more she thought about it, the more she realised her own ambitions were starting to take shape too.

When Lily had come into her life, the most rewarding part had been gaining the little mare's trust and becoming her friend. The rosettes, the horsey fame and the championship titles had been amazing, but really they were just the icing on the cake. She knew the little mare was phenomenally talented. Janey, who had followed the palomino's progress from the start, wouldn't have put her name forward for the week otherwise. Once again, Georgia said a silent thank-you to Melanie for not selling Lily on for thousands of pounds as she could have, but letting Georgia keep her at Redgrove Farm instead.

Redgrove Farm. It was where she was happiest, just mucking out, riding over the downs and hanging out in the tack room with her friends. But was Lily's talent wasted there? Or was a pony ever really wasted, if they were loved and happy? Maybe Georgia didn't need to push Lily any further. Placing her arms round the little mare's warm neck, she rested her head against her, breathing in her unique pony scent. She would see the week through, there was no doubt about that, if only to prove Henry and Serena wrong and stick by Jodie. But who knew what would happen after that!

The next day's riding was altogether more positive. During the group lesson, Georgia, Jodie and Ellie were coached by Daisy while Serena and Sebastian worked in the lower half of the school under Henry's instruction. Daisy was a brilliant instructor, kind but firm and with an excellent eye for detail. She reminded Georgia of Melanie. Soon Georgia and Lily were performing the most fantastic collected canter – something she had never attempted before. Daisy just knew how to ask the ponies to perform and Georgia was amazed at how the smallest of changes, the quietest of nudges in just the right place, could get

Lily dancing as she had never danced before. Her extended trot was longer and more powerful than ever, and her canter, as slow as walking pace, was perfection.

Georgia couldn't stop grinning. Despite her thoughts from the previous evening, when she had realised she didn't have the competitive streak that Jodie had, it didn't mean she didn't want to learn new riding skills and so she soaked up Daisy's words like a sponge. Jodie and Ellie looked happy for the first time as well.

While the girls rode together, Georgia had her first glimpse at just how tricky Jackson could be. When Jodie asked for a flying change, Jackson plunged to the side, nostrils flaring, before wheeling round and half rearing, the whites of his eyes flashing. Georgia admired the way that Jodie hardly moved in the saddle, not panicking in the slightest. Instead she circled the glossy black pony, patting him on the neck and scratching his withers while talking to him in a low voice. Relaxing again, Jackson performed the perfect flying change.

"Well done!" Daisy seemed thrilled at their progress. Despite the chill, Georgia had already discarded her jacket. Who knew flatwork could be such hot work? She felt as though she had been for a ten-mile run! She patted Lily, proud of herself and the palomino, and relieved she was proving she deserved her place.

"Well done, everyone!" Daisy beamed again. "Now," she continued, giving all three ponies a pat. "Rosefolly is going to get quite exciting from now on." She leaned in towards the pupils. "We have someone joining us tomorrow," Daisy said with a smile. "Someone very important!"

Georgia and Jodie exchanged glances as Daisy went on to explain that a team selector for the Young Riders Dressage Squad was coming to watch the teens in the build-up to the assessment day. The final day would be the official assessment, but observations would be made up until then. They would be assisted, Daisy explained, her sunny smile vanishing for just a split second as she glanced over at the other group, by Henry Winters.

Jodie's shoulders slumped, and Ellie gave a small groan. If Henry was involved, Georgia realised, Jodie wouldn't get a chance to shine. She needed to help her!

☆ ☆ ☆

Once riding was done for the day, Georgia tried to get Jodie on her own. She knew that tomorrow would be Jodie's big chance, and she didn't want her to worry about Serena. Skipping out of Lily's stable before teatime, she paused, leaning her head against her shavings fork. She could hear hushed, angry voices, and was straining to work out where they were coming from when Jodie appeared in

Jackson's stable next door. Putting her fingers to her lips, Georgia gestured to Jodie to stay quiet, so she could work out what was being said. Jodie stood as still as a statue against Jackson's neck, her face turning pale. The voices belonged to Serena and Henry. Clearly they had thought everyone would be in the canteen for tea.

Serena sounded angry and Henry was trying to placate her. "You said she wouldn't be a problem!" Her flat, polished voice rose slightly as she talked.

"Don't worry." Henry's clipped tones were instantly recognisable. "I'll take care of it. There's no way Jodie will ride if she knows I can sack Amanda."

"Then why is she still here?" Serena's voice was a whine now.

"Leave it to me." Henry's voice was cross. "I said I'd sort it!"

Jodie remained as still as before, long after Serena

and Henry had exited the barn, their footsteps ringing out against the cobbles.

"Well, that's it then," she whispered finally. "I'm not going to let Mum lose her job again."

Georgia didn't know what to say. After all, Henry was in charge while the owners of the centre were thousands of miles away. Why was he so keen to get Serena on the young riders' squad, even at the expense of an innocent groom's job? He must know there were other riders more deserving of a place.

"I'm going to get to the bottom of this," Georgia said firmly to her friend, who only shrugged her shoulders, biting her lip as she tried not to cry. Seeing Jodie's crumpled face only strengthened Georgia's resolve to find out exactly what was going on.

CHAPTER EIGHT

"Have you heard?" Sebastian clearly couldn't wait to spill the beans the next morning at breakfast as he wolfed down his cereal. "Ellie's left!"

Georgia just gaped at him, and Jodie did the same as Serena sat down next to Sebastian. Georgia could have sworn a look of satisfaction flickered across Serena's face.

"Couldn't hack it; always wondered why she

was here," she said dismissively.

Georgia felt a bubble of anger grow, thinking of poor Ellie who had been pulled apart by Henry during the very first lesson. "That's not fair!" she cried. "Ellie was a great rider, and she had as good a chance as any of us at getting a squad place!"

"Oh, well, one down." Serena was as cold as ice, and even Sebastian looked slightly shocked as Serena continued. "We're finding out who can *really* take the pace, I guess."

Georgia was just about to retort when she felt Jodie's elbow prodding her, and kept her mouth shut. Remembering their overheard conversation in the stables last night, Georgia's eyes narrowed. Serena was playing dirty, and Henry was helping her. Georgia believed he would quite easily sack the loyal groom if Jodie didn't give up her place on the course. She had no evidence of this but she didn't trust Serena or Henry one bit. She had to do something. Finding she had totally lost her appetite, she pushed her chair back and stood up. She wished Melanie or Dan were here – they always knew what to do.

She remembered what Jodie had told her about Martha and James, the owners of Rosefolly. If only they knew what was going on while they were away. Then she had a brainwave. Rosefolly's owners may be in Australia but that didn't mean Georgia couldn't contact them. She needed Jodie to know she could ride for her chance of glory without worrying about her mum's job.

Running back up to her dorm room, she pulled out her old laptop, which she had brought with her to appease her own mum, promising that she would get some coursework done in the evenings. Feeling slightly guilty as she realised she hadn't done any work at all, she turned it on, drumming her fingers against the keyboard impatiently. She went on to the Rosefolly website, quickly finding the email address for James and Martha Davidson, proprietors of Rosefolly Equestrian Centre. She paused as she thought about what to write.

Dear Mr and Mrs Davidson.

Her fingers hovered over the keyboard.

My name is Georgia Black and I am currently training at Rosefolly. I am sorry to contact you while you are so far away, but I hope you can help me. I am worried Henry Winters may be threatening to sack your groom Amanda, to stop her daughter Jodie from trying out for a squad place. I need to let Jodie know that he can't do that. Thank you, Georgia May Black.

Pressing 'Send', Georgia crossed her fingers before rushing back down to the stable block.

As the adrenalin of what she had done wore off, she pressed her face into Lily's neck, her cheeks crimson. Had she done the right thing? She didn't even know Rosefolly's owners, and she had got involved with something she shouldn't have. They were probably going to be furious at Georgia for contacting them; maybe they would even get Henry to throw her off the course. She felt her whole body tingle hot and cold with shame. As Lily snuffled her hands in slight alarm, picking up on her young mistress's emotions, Georgia groaned. She could only hope for the best; she couldn't go back on what she had just done.

☆ ☆ ☆

The team selector who arrived at the yard the next day was a kindly-looking older man in cord trousers and a sponsor's blouson jacket. He looked as though he had been around horses all his life as he strolled up and down the arena, taking in

each pony and rider as they stood quietly. Georgia had spent an extra few minutes turning Lily out so that she looked particularly smart, and her neat pale feet were polished and her mane fell in soft creamy waves. She was so pretty, so understated, in her simple snaffle bridle. Georgia still wasn't sure how she felt about going further with Lily but that didn't mean she wasn't going to try her best, as she had promised Mel.

She noticed that the team selector spent a couple of extra minutes looking at Jackson and Lily, and her blood ran cold as she noticed the look of rage crossing Henry's face. He really wanted Serena to make the squad. But why?

For the rest of the lesson, the team selector stood quietly, occasionally making notes but mostly just leaning on the fence observing the riders. Henry seemed determined that Serena would be noticed, and stood Georgia and Jodie right at the back of the arena as Serena and her chestnut pony ran through a dressage test. Georgia tried to gauge the look on the team selector's face, but it was totally unreadable. Georgia wondered if the expectation was extra high on Serena due to her famous father, and for the briefest of seconds she felt a smidgen of pity towards her. It couldn't be easy – especially as she seemed to lack natural talent. But then, remembering the way Serena was trying to shove everyone off the course, she frowned. She didn't feel *that* sorry for her!

"Have you seen enough?" Henry was desperately trying to bring the session to a close, but Georgia and Jodie had barely even ridden a circle. It was deliberate sabotage, Georgia thought angrily.

"Not quite." The team selector glanced at his watch as he answered. "Can I just see the palomino and the black pony in action?"

"Of course," Henry said through gritted teeth.

"But if you ask me," he said in a stage whisper, "the palomino is all flash, no substance, and the black pony is far too unpredictable, dangerous even."

"I'll be the judge of that," the team selector said in a level voice, flicking through his notepad. "The pony's got a good record at competitions, I see here."

Henry snorted. "Only local stuff, nothing to speak of. A Blackpool donkey would win a prize at some of the shows round here." With that he called Georgia and Jodie forward, his eyes flashing. Georgia nudged Lily forward and the little mare sprang into action. She made sure that she gave Jodie plenty of space, knowing Jackson was prone to explosions if other ponies got too close, and concentrated on showing off her little mare's paces – a walk-to-canter transition and a perfect leg yield.

Glancing over at Jodie and Jackson, she frowned. Something was wrong. Jodie was holding Jackson back, causing him to pin his ears back in frustration and throw in little bunny hops. Silently, Georgia willed Jodie to really show her gelding off. What was going wrong? Then, to her horror, she realised that Jodie must be deliberately sabotaging her chance. She must really believe that Henry would sack her mum if Serena didn't get the place. Georgia could only watch helplessly as Jodie held her hand up and asked if she could stop riding, much to the team selector's confusion.

"I don't want to ride any more," Jodie said in a trembling voice, much to Serena's barely concealed delight and Henry's satisfaction as he turned back to the team selector.

"What did I say?" His flat haughty voice carried over the arena to Georgia. "The pony's too unpredictable and the girl knows it. Not like this

84

one." He gestured to Serena's chestnut.

The team selector frowned. "Very well," he replied as he turned to go. "But I want to watch some more before making a choice. We've still got the rest of the week, haven't we?" And without a backward glance he turned on his heel and strode away from the yard.

CHAPTER NINE

"What was that all about?" Georgia tried to talk to Jodie as they untacked their ponies next to each other in the huge stone stables. But from the way Jodie hunched her shoulders over Jackson, her hat pulled down low, it was clear she wasn't in a talking mood. Georgia knew she had ridden badly on purpose, and felt a growing bubble of anger rise against Henry and Serena. Georgia was so wrapped up in Jodie and Jackson that she hadn't even stopped to wonder if the team selector had been impressed with her and Lily, although Lily had felt as good as ever. She scratched the little mare on her withers and Lily lowered her lovely pale eyelashes. She still wasn't sure what her aim was for the week, but one thing was for sure – she was going to stick it out, if only to make sure Jodie was OK.

"I'm going home for the rest of the day," Jodie muttered, concentrating hard on Jackson's saddle as she undid his girth. Before Georgia could make any further attempt at conversation, she heard her name being called. It was Daisy. Looking round her stable door, she saw the assistant instructor standing in the doorway to the barn. She had her arms folded and looked very serious. Georgia felt her cheeks flush. It had to be about the email she had sent Rosefolly's owners. She had a feeling she was in deep trouble.

Giving Lily a pat, she let herself out of the stable and walked towards the instructor with trepidation, her legs trembling.

"Follow me," Daisy said grimly, and Georgia meekly trotted behind her to the instructor's office. Thankfully there was no sign of Henry. Georgia couldn't bear it if he was witness to her telling-off – it was bad enough she had let the friendly and knowledgeable Daisy down. Imagining what she was going to tell Melanie and Janey, Georgia felt her hands grow sweaty.

Daisy shut the door and sat down behind the desk, and Georgia stood awkwardly, one ankle behind the other, awaiting her fate.

"Did you contact James and Martha Davidson?" Daisy looked straight at Georgia, unblinking, and Georgia lowered her head.

"Yes," she whispered. "I wanted to let them know

how badly Henry and Serena were behaving." She may as well tell the truth if she was going to get kicked off the course.

There was a long silence, only broken by the ticking of a clock on the huge antique desk.

"I'm glad," Daisy said finally, to Georgia's surprise, and she looked up at Daisy, who smiled at her kindly. "You're not in trouble, Georgia. Don't look so worried." Daisy explained that she had also suspected something was going on between Serena and Henry, and had done some digging of her own. She knew the groom at the Van der Hawks' yard, who had taken over from Amanda when she had left. The groom had confirmed Henry was heavily involved with Serena's father's horse-dealing business. Daisy could only presume Henry was being bribed in order to get Serena a squad place, either by forcing everyone else off the course, or by threatening Jodie's mum with the sack if Jodie didn't pull out.

When James, the owner of Rosefolly, had called Daisy just after today's lesson to discuss Georgia's email, Daisy had filled him in on what was happening.

"I've told James everything," said Daisy. "And this is what he wants us to do. We've got to persuade Jodie to carry on. James has given his word that Amanda's job is safe, and he will investigate Henry as soon as he's back in the UK."

"But will Jodie believe that?" Georgia asked.

"Let's hope so," Daisy said grimly. "I'll have a word with her." Then, smiling, she opened the door for Georgia. "Tell you what," she said, her face sunny again. "The team selector isn't back until tomorrow. We *could* have a lesson, but what do you say to a hack around the estate, just you, me and Jodie? I can bring my horse; he's stabled on the main yard."

"Brilliant!" Georgia grinned. She couldn't think of a better idea. After all the pressure of the first part of the course, a relaxed hack would do her and Lily the world of good.

"Great, then meet me at two under the archway. I'll take care of Henry." Daisy smiled. Then she looked straight at Georgia. "Oh, I nearly forgot to tell you, what with everything going on," she said. "Alongside Jodie and Jackson, you and Lily have the most potential I have seen in a long, long time. The partnership between you is amazing. That pony could take you right to the top, Georgia."

Georgia could only gape in astonishment as she followed Daisy into the sunlit yard. And here she was, wanting to get back to Redgrove and Pony Club rallies. Should she really be aiming higher? Lily was a one-in-a-million pony, that was certain. But Georgia had to think carefully about the path she chose. As she walked out of the office, she nearly bumped headlong into Jodie.

"What was that about?" her friend asked her.

"I'll explain later," Georgia said. "But, Jodie, you mustn't leave! Daisy knows what Henry is up to and she's spoken to the owner of Rosefolly. Just promise me you'll come out for a hack with Daisy and me, and we'll tell you everything."

"OK." Jodie looked intrigued. "I've half packed my trunk, but Mum's working all afternoon anyway so I can't move Jackson back to his livery yard until tomorrow. A ride out sounds just what I need – it has to be better than seeing the look of smug satisfaction on Serena's face for the rest of the day."

"Great," Georgia grinned. "Two o'clock, under the archway!"

☆ ☆ ☆

There was something quite pleasing about riding out through the gates of Rosefolly later that afternoon. Serena was clearly convinced that Jodie was giving up and that Georgia would follow. The look of satisfaction on her face as she led her chestnut pony out of his stable was almost too much to bear. Luckily, Daisy distracted Georgia, leading out the most beautiful grey thoroughbred from one of Rosefolly's plush boxes.

"Thanks, Amanda," Georgia heard her say to Jodie's mum, who held her stirrup on one side so that Daisy could lightly swing into the saddle. "She always does such a good job, your mum." She smiled at Jodie, who looked pleased.

Daisy's horse, Louis, was an ex-racehorse. Daisy had bought the gelding and slowly nursed him back to health after an injury, and he had rewarded her by winning major dressage titles and showing classes for ex-racehorses. He had even been to the Horse of the Year Show. Riding little Lily next to the big handsome grey, Georgia decided

Daisy could be added to her list of horsey heroes!

The trio laughed and chatted easily as the path soon gave way to the rolling parkland surrounding Rosefolly, dotted with grazing sheep and, to Georgia's immense surprise, tame deer that looked up in mild interest as the horses passed by. Lily was completely on her toes, spooking slightly at the deer, making Georgia laugh, her lovely ears pricked forward. Georgia realised it was the happiest she had been all week.

As they rode, Daisy explained clearly to Jodie about what she suspected was going on between Serena and Henry. Jodie was completely quiet, absorbing Daisy's words. Georgia stayed slightly behind, but was still able to hear what was being said.

"So Mum's job is safe?" Jodie kept asking.

Daisy told her that she knew there had to be a

reason why Henry was so desperate for Serena to get the coveted place. It still wasn't exactly clear, but all Jodie was interested in was that Henry wouldn't be able to sack her mum, and that Jodie could still ride.

Daisy nodded. "Absolutely," she said firmly. "You need to get back on the horse, as it were, and show the selectors what you're made of!"

Jodie nodded back. "OK," she agreed. "If you're sure."

Georgia smiled, still slightly behind the two riders, and patted Lily's glossy neck. She was thrilled; Jodie deserved her chance to ride without being intimidated. She wondered what reason there could be for Henry trying to push her off, but she didn't really care, as long as Daisy was sure Jodie could still ride and that Amanda's job was safe.

Daisy turned round in the saddle, reins in one

hand, and grinned at Georgia. "There's the most perfect piece of flat ground just up ahead," she said, her eyes sparkling. "It's where I often school Louis, for a change of scene. What do you say to a bit of a practice, before tomorrow?"

Both girls smiled in agreement.

Away from the confines of the arena, Lily felt so free and responsive, and with Daisy sitting in the middle of the circle on a relaxed Louis, the two young teenagers flourished under her instruction, both Jackson and Lily trotting perfect serpentines and a balanced counter canter. Georgia laughed in delight as Lily flew into the most amazing extended canter. She never knew she could ride like this, and marvelled once again at how the smallest changes could make the biggest difference.

As the three rode their weary horses back down into Rosefolly, the afternoon light fading and the temperature dropping, Georgia felt a huge sense of the

PALOMINO
✿PONY

relief. It had been a bit risky, emailing Rosefolly's owners, but her gamble had paid off. Now all they had to do was ride like never before.

CHAPTER TEN

The positive energy from the previous afternoon's schooling session in the parkland carried over to the next morning as Georgia and Jodie joined Serena and Sebastian for breakfast. The first thing Georgia noticed was that Serena had a face like thunder, and Henry wasn't sitting in his normal place at the front of the room. There was no way she was going to ask where he was, so she was relieved when

Sebastian looked round in confusion.

"Where's Henry?" he asked, pausing between mouthfuls of toast and marmalade.

"He's not here today," Serena spat, shooting a murderous look at Georgia and Jodie.

Georgia shivered slightly, but held her ground. Rosefolly's owners must have been in contact with him. Georgia was relieved. Without Henry around, both she and Jodie could relax, and Jodie in particular could ride to the best of her abilities without Henry constantly picking on her. If Daisy was in charge of the instruction, the playing field was level.

"Has he gone for good?" Georgia asked quietly.

"He'll be back for the assessment day," Serena said icily, "but we've got to put up with that drip Daisy until then."

Georgia decided it was better to keep her mouth shut at this point, but inside she felt like dancing, and practically ran to the stables after breakfast to get Lily tacked up in time for the morning lesson.

✩ ✪ ✩

The team selector, Richard, was coming back that morning to observe the group. It was the last time he'd be there until Friday – assessment day – with the rest of the panel. Then they would choose the rider for the squad place. Georgia realised Serena was hoping both Jodie and Georgia would have been pushed out by then, like Ellie. She felt quite triumphant knowing the spoiled teenager hadn't won.

With Daisy in charge of the lesson, everyone got a fair chance at riding. Even Serena had an equal chance, but Georgia reflected on how her riding paled against Jodie's, now that Jodie wasn't afraid to really show her skills off. They were working on transitions and accuracy, and soon all four students were perfecting a walk-to-canter movement. Daisy

was very like Melanie in her way of teaching,
believing in getting the basics right first, and
Georgia could feel herself soaking up her words
like a sponge. Without really trying, she and Lily
were growing stronger and better as a partnership.
She loved seeing Jodie looking so happy, with her
lovely black pony dancing across the arena. Jackson
really was something special. No wonder Serena
was so angry that she wasn't able to ride him. With
Jodie riding so beautifully, she and Jackson really
had to be a serious contender for the squad place.

✿ ✿ ✿

Curled up on Lily's rug later, Georgia stretched
her stiff legs. All her muscles were aching and she
rubbed the back of her shin as she dialled Dan's
number. She really missed him, and felt a pang of
homesickness. There was no reply on his mobile,
and she looked at her phone in disappointment.
Feeling brave, she dialled his house number,

crossing her fingers that he picked up. Ben, Dan's older brother, answered instead with a cheerful hello. "Hi ... it's Georgia," she said shyly, although she was never sure why she felt shy – Ben and Mr Coleman were both really nice, even more so after Georgia's rescue of the farm sheep!

"Hey, Georgia!" Ben said, chatting happily. "How's Lily? Off to the Olympics yet?"

Georgia smiled. "Not quite," she said, as Ben chuckled. After exchanging a couple of pleasantries about the farm and the ponies, Georgia asked if Dan was about.

"No... Oh, let me see." Georgia could practically hear Ben shake his head as he continued. "He's helping Dad with the milking."

Georgia glanced at her watch; it was a bit early for the afternoon milking. "OK, thanks," she said, feeling slightly deflated. She had really been hoping to talk to Dan, to ask his advice on how she was feeling about Lily and the assessment day. "Tell him I rang."

Turning back to Lily, Georgia placed her arms round her glossy cream neck, enjoying the sound of the little mare munching on her hay net. They both jumped as her phone rang a minute later. Pulling it out, she squinted at the screen and smiled. Dan.

"Hey, G!" Dan sounded slightly out of breath, and Georgia could hear the wind whistling around the phone. "Sorry I missed your call. I was out running."

"Oh, right." Georgia frowned. "I just spoke to Ben, and he said you were milking with your dad."

There was the briefest of pauses before Dan laughed.

"Oh, he just got confused, probably. I dunno," he blustered cheerfully.

Georgia raised an eyebrow, not that Dan could

see it. She didn't want to appear suspicious, but when had Dan ever gone running? Maybe with Georgia gone he was starting to do other things: football, running, and maybe even meeting Becky Hanbury, who was *still* desperate to go out with him.

After they said goodbye, Georgia hung up, feeling slightly upset. Thank goodness for Lily, who stopped eating her hay to rest her head on Georgia's shoulder, leaving a trail of white froth. Georgia hugged the little mare back. Only a couple of days left and she would be home. She just had to stop her imagination from running away with her before then.

But her fears were soon made worse that evening. Ringing Emma, she mentioned that Dan had said he was busy earlier that day.

"Oh, yes," Emma said cheerfully. "He was out with Will."

"Will?" Georgia was really confused now. "Ben said he was milking, Dan said he was running… Em, what's going on?"

"Nothing, honestly, G," Emma said trying to reassure her friend.

"You would tell me, wouldn't you," Georgia said, "if there was something I needed to know?"

"Course!" Emma answered hotly, sounding slightly irritated, and seemingly keen not to talk about Dan. "Anyway, you need to hear about my cinema trip with Will. So he said…"

As Emma nattered away about her date and Redgrove and normal life, Georgia frowned. Emma was her best friend. She would tell her if Dan was up to something, wouldn't she?

CHAPTER ELEVEN

After a sleepless night worrying about both home and the assessment day, Georgia tried hard to push any worrying thoughts about Dan's strange behaviour to the back of her mind. The four riders had only one day left of training and the air was electric with anticipation. Who would be chosen? Serena was silent throughout breakfast, glowering over her bowl of cereal, but Sebastian was in a jovial mood, chatting away to Georgia and Jodie.

"Jackson's going really well," he smiled at Jodie, who blushed, shrinking away, as Serena shot her a foul look.

"He's too unreliable," Serena practically spat at Jodie.

"Oh, I don't know," Sebastian said, stretching. "He looks like he's going really great to me. You ride brilliantly, Jodie." He smiled at Jodie, his teeth very straight and white, and Jodie's cheeks burned a bright scarlet, much to Georgia's amusement. Maybe Sebastian was starting to see through Serena after all.

Once breakfast was cleared, Georgia and Jodie walked arm in arm to the pony block. Georgia had a feeling Jodie would be a friend for life now, and was so glad she was staying for the assessment day. If Jodie rode like she had yesterday, she had a really good chance.

"*And so do you*," she heard a small voice inside her say. It was so confusing. The more she was told how good Lily was, the more she wondered whether she should really try for a place herself. But at the same time she missed Redgrove, even more so after Emma's phone call last night. She had enjoyed the lessons during her time at Rosefolly, but she had enjoyed the impromptu hack most of all. Olympia and the Horse of the Year Show had been amazing, but mainly because of how far Lily had come. The gaining of her trust, the schooling and the bonding had been her favourite parts of Lily's journey, and the rosettes at Olympia had just been proof of that. Would Lily be better off with someone who could take her right to the top, and push her even further? Georgia just didn't know.

Deep in thought, she set to work grooming Lily for the day's lessons. No matter how many times she did it, Georgia still loved grooming Lily and she always took her time over it, carefully body-brushing Lily's golden coat and combing out her creamy mane. A lick of hoof oil finished off the look.

"Pretty as a picture," Georgia grinned, giving the palomino a kiss on her velvet muzzle. Just as she was doing up the chinstrap of her riding hat, she heard Jodie's panicked voice next door.

"Georgia?" Jodie's voice was shrill and tense.

Giving Lily a pat, Georgia went to investigate after tying the little mare back up. "Georgia, something's wrong with Jackson!" Jodie sounded close to tears.

Georgia leaned over the stable door, observing the handsome black gelding. Jackson looked at healthy as ever but Jodie was right, he was favouring his near fore, shifting the weight so that he could rest it.

"I was picking out his feet," Jodie explained,

"but he seemed really tender on that foot." She gestured to the hoof.

"Have you trotted him up?" Georgia asked, trying to think rationally.

Jodie shook her head. "No," she said miserably. "But here's Daisy. I wonder if she can watch him move."

The assistant instructor joined the girls in the stable, agreeing that Jackson was favouring his front leg. "Trot him up," she said firmly and, giving Jackson a pat, Jodie led the black gelding out into the frosty yard. Daisy stood with her hands on her knees, watching carefully as Jodie encouraged Jackson to trot towards her in a straight line. The slight nodding head and uneven gait made Georgia wince. The pony was definitely lame. "Well, there's no heat and no swelling. I'd make a likely guess it's his foot," Daisy observed as she ran a hand down Jackson's slim legs. "The vet's coming this morning to check on one of the foals. I'll get him to see you before he does that."

Jodie nodded miserably. Feeling awful, Georgia carried on tacking up Lily, crossing her fingers there was nothing seriously wrong with Jackson.

The vet, a smartly dressed man in a navy waistcoat and mustard cords, was soon checking Jackson.

Picking up his foot, the vet examined it carefully, feeling for any sore spots. His pincers must have hit the tender area because Jackson visibly winced.

"Bruised sole, I'm fairly sure," the vet said cheerfully. "A few days' rest should sort it."

Jodie was obviously relieved Jackson was going to be OK but her face crumpled with disappointment. Her chance of a squad place was rapidly disappearing if she wasn't going to be able to ride during the assessment day. Biting her lip, she placed a hand on Jackson's neck to steady herself. "But how?" she whispered miserably. "He was fine last night, and he's been in his stable since then."

"Well, horses do find ways to injure themselves." The vet shrugged, packing up his case. "Perhaps have a good check in his bed, just in case. In the meantime, box rest, a hot poultice and I'll prescribe the poor chap some painkillers. But he'll be right as rain in a few days."

Once the vet had gone to make his checks on the foal, Jodie started burrowing frantically in Jackson's deep shavings bed.

"What are you doing?" Georgia said curiously.

"You heard what he said," Jodie replied, looking carefully through the bedding. "I *know* Jackson was fine last night." Scraping the shavings aside with her hands, she suddenly leaned back on her haunches, clutching a small object. "Eureka!" she said grimly. "How did this get here?" She held the

112

object aloft for Georgia to inspect. It was a stone of some sort, creamy white, with shiny darker grey bits. The sharp edges made Georgia wince as she realised what it was. "A flint," Jodie said darkly, examining it. "In my pony's bed. And now he's lame. Georgia, this isn't a coincidence!"

CHAPTER TWELVE

"Oh, what a shame!" Serena flicked her dark hair over her shoulder as she led her chestnut gelding past the stable. He was kept in the adjacent block but she had to pass Georgia and Jodie on the way to the outdoor school. "Daisy told me what happened," she said, sounding totally insincere. "You should probably work on your mucking-out technique."

Georgia could have sworn Serena was smirking as she ran her stirrups down, and couldn't contain herself. "It was you, wasn't it!" she hissed at Serena, who merely raised an eyebrow.

"Dear, dear," Serena tutted. "Be careful who you go around accusing, Georgia." Her eyes narrowed as she mounted her chestnut pony and wheeled him in the direction of the outdoor school.

"I'm sorry, Jodie," Georgia said, watching Jodie burying her head in Jackson's mane. "I shouldn't have said anything."

Georgia knew she shouldn't have flown off the handle like that. It was possible the flint could have innocently found its way into the stable; the fields were full of them, after all. Still, nothing could change the fact that poor Jackson was lame and would be out of action for the next few days. For Jodie, it meant her dream of a funded-rider place had shattered into a million pieces. The rules were clear; the riders had to be mounted for the assessment day. Georgia didn't think she could feel any more sorry for Jodie as she gently led Lily out of her stable.

"I won't ride." She hesitated at the entrance to the barn, looking back at her friend, who stood close to Jackson looking totally dejected. "I'll stay with you if you want."

But Jodie shook her head firmly, insisting Georgia join the lesson. "I'll be fine," she said miserably. "Mum's doing a long day today but she can take Jackson home tonight. I guess that's that." She hesitated. "Georgia, you need to ride for both of us now. We can't let Serena win!"

✩ ✩ ✩

Without Jodie in the lesson, Georgia found her mind wandering. She tried hard to concentrate on what Daisy was telling her, but couldn't stop thinking about poor Jodie. Although horses had a reputation for laming themselves at the worst possible times, Georgia was certain it was no accident.

As Georgia pushed Lily into an extended trot, it hit her like a ton of bricks. No matter how many people told her Lily could go further, Georgia knew that she simply didn't have the drive or determination that Jodie had. She just wasn't hungry for it. She would be happier cantering over the downs with Will, or trotting down the lanes with Emma. But Jodie was different. Not only was she a fantastic rider who loved her pony, but she had the drive and talent to succeed. Georgia knew she would go far if she just had the chance.

As she cooled Lily down after the lesson, a plan was beginning to take shape in her mind. But first she needed to talk to the one person who always knew what was best for her and Lily.

✫ ✬ ✫

Sometimes life had a funny way of working out, and as Georgia sat down for lunch one of the grooms scurried in with a message for her. Following her to the office, Georgia gave a start as she saw Melanie and Sophie waiting for her, both smiling from ear to ear.

"Mel!" Giving them both a big hug, Georgia turned to the owner of Redgrove Farm. "What are you doing here?" She smiled.

Melanie grinned. She explained that she was on her way to drop Sophie back at university after a reading week, but as they were close to Rosefolly they'd decided to pop in and see how Georgia and Lily were getting on.

"Wow, it's something else here, isn't it?" Sophie whistled, gazing around her.

Georgia had to admit Rosefolly did look amazing in the winter sunshine. "Yes, it's gorgeous,"

Georgia agreed. "And it's been . . . interesting."

"Let's go and say hello to Lily." Melanie smiled at Georgia, sensing something was up. "And you can tell me all about your week."

"OK." Georgia agreed, still over the moon at seeing them but feeling slightly nervous about what she was about to ask Melanie.

As they turned the corner to the box, Lily was also overjoyed to see Sophie and Melanie, whickering in recognition and nodding her head.

"Oh, she looks great, Georgia." Melanie ran her hand down Lily's silken mane, patting her strong neck. "What do you think your chances are for the assessment day?"

Georgia swallowed. After the build-up to the Horse of the Year Show, when Georgia hadn't been honest about how nervous she felt, she knew she had to be totally upfront with Mel. So she tried to explain how she really felt – that she didn't want to push Lily any harder and that she didn't have that burning ambition to take it further. Saying it out loud only confirmed it.

"The thing is, I already feel like the luckiest girl in the world, looking after Lily. I just want to enjoy her. I only want to do the odd show, maybe the pony club teams. I feel like Lily doesn't have anything else to prove now." Looking up, Georgia saw Sophie was smiling, but Melanie looked thoughtful. "Are you disappointed?" Georgia asked quietly.

"Well, I'd be lying if I said I wasn't a little bit," Melanie said gently. "But, Georgia, it's your choice. You're the one who rides her. If you don't want to go further, that's for you to decide." She patted Lily on her golden neck. "Why don't we have a good talk about things when you get back to Redgrove?"

"OK," said Georgia, not really knowing what

Melanie meant, but agreeing to it all the same. But there was still something Georgia wanted to ask her. A plan had been forming in her mind. While Mel and Sophie listened, Georgia explained Jodie's predicament and the fact she had no pony to ride for the assessment day. Georgia had checked the rules several times after her morning lessons, and there was nothing to say a candidate couldn't ride a borrowed pony for the trial but be partnered with their own pony going forward.

"So you want to give up your place at the assessment?" Sophie said quietly, "and let this Jodie girl ride Lily?"

Georgia nodded as she shrugged her shoulders. "I know, you think I'm mad," she said with a small smile. "But Jodie really, really deserves a chance."

"How do you feel about someone else riding Lily?" Melanie frowned.

"I wouldn't suggest it if I didn't trust her,"

Georgia replied honestly. "She's one of the best riders I've ever seen. But it's really up to you. You're her official owner."

Melanie turned to Lily and patted the little mare, her face thoughtful. "Well, I've always trusted you, Georgia," she said finally. "If you think it's the right thing to do, then I'll be behind you." She looked at her watch. "What do you think, Sophie?" she asked her daughter. "Can we spare a couple of hours to watch the lesson this afternoon?"

"Defo," Sophie grinned. "I was only going to go to the library ... although I promise I'll make up for it another time, Mum!" she added hastily as her mum raised an eyebrow.

"Great!" Georgia said. She hoped that once Melanie and Sophie had watched Jodie ride, they would agree that Georgia was doing the right thing. For just a moment, she hesitated. If she let Jodie take the ride tomorrow on the assessment day, there was no going back. But Georgia felt happy with her decision not to take Lily further. All Georgia had ever wanted was her very own pony, and Lily had fulfilled that dream and more.

Melanie placed her hand on her arm, sensing Georgia's hesitation. "Are you sure? You have thought about what you're giving up, haven't you?" she asked quietly, her tone serious.

Georgia nodded her head vigorously. She had never been more certain about anything. Now all she needed to do was convince Jodie!

Chapter Thirteen

"Lily?" Jodie was as surprised as Georgia thought she would be when she, Melanie and Sophie went to find her in the main tack room on the yard, where she was sharing a cup of tea with her mum. "You want me to ride Lily?" she repeated slowly.

"Yes," Georgia said, nodding, "but only if you want to."

Jodie just stared at her. "But if I ride..." she said

finally, "that means you give up your chance?"

"Yes," Georgia repeated, smiling. "I've thought it over a million times, and I just don't want to go any further with Lily. I love the showing, I really do, but all I ever wanted was a pony to call my own, and that's Lily." She shrugged helplessly as she continued. "I never set out to get to Olympia; it just sort of happened. Honestly, I'd rather take Lily back home tomorrow and just go for a hack."

"Wow." It was clear from Jodie's face that she was still trying to process Georgia's offer.

The two girls were silent for a minute as Jodie fiddled with the mug she was holding, before her face dissolved into an ear-to-ear grin and she leapt up to hug Georgia. "Well, if you're quite sure then I'd be honoured," she said laughing. "Thank you so much!"

✿ ✪ ✿

Once Jodie had agreed to ride Lily, things started

to move quickly. Melanie and Sophie stayed at Rosefolly for the afternoon. Georgia couldn't be more pleased to have them there with her but she still wasn't sure how Melanie really felt about Georgia not riding in the assessment. What if Melanie thought Georgia was being ungrateful, after all the help she had received at Redgrove? Lily had so much talent, and yet here was Georgia saying that she just wanted to take her home for hacking and Pony Club!

When Daisy came to take Jodie and Lily for one last lesson, Sophie told Georgia all about Santa, and Callie's latest escape into the tack room back at Redgrove. It made Georgia laugh out loud. She really did miss everything and everyone back home.

"Has Dan been around much?" Georgia tried to ask as casually as possible.

"Dan?"

Was it Georgia's imagination or did Sophie look slightly startled for a second? "Um, I don't think so," Sophie said finally. "I've hardly seen him at all." She furrowed her brows as if trying to remember if she had actually seen Dan at all in recent days.

Georgia felt her heart sink. Dan had told her he was hanging out with Will loads, and Emma had said this too. Ben had said he was working on the farm, and now Sophie said she hadn't seen him at all! There was definitely something going on. There was no point ringing or texting; she may as well wait until she was home to find out.

Sophie quickly changed the subject, confirming Georgia's fears. Dan was *definitely* up to something.

✰ ✰ ✰

After a quick lunch with Mel and Sophie, Georgia leaned on the arena fence, feeling the weak sunshine warm her face. At least Mel had seemed happy with the way Jodie had ridden Lily, but it was hard to know what she was really thinking about Georgia's big decision. For Georgia it had been the strangest thing ever, grooming and tacking Lily up as normal, but then handing the reins over to someone else.

Luckily, because Jodie had stabled Jackson next to the little mare throughout the week, Lily was familiar with Jodie's gentle voice and had stood quietly as Jodie lightly swung herself into the saddle and adjusted the stirrups, her legs far longer than Georgia's.

She trotted Lily forward and Georgia felt a lump rise in her throat. Jodie rode so beautifully – together the two of them made a perfect picture. For just a second Georgia wondered if Lily would be better off with someone else – someone who would take her further. But deep down, she knew Lily loved life at Redgrove as much as she did, and that ponies didn't need glory and applause to be happy. They didn't mind if they were trotting up the centre line at the Olympics or just riding around the village once a week, so long as they were loved and well looked after.

As Georgia watched, she found herself enjoying the lesson a lot more than she thought she would. There was something very rewarding about watching Lily perform a perfect extended trot with another rider, knowing it was Georgia's own hard work that had got her to that point.

She was so totally transfixed watching the little mare that she didn't notice the look of fury on Serena's face at first. Serena dug her heels into the handsome chestnut's sides, clearly frustrated that Jodie was outriding her. As Georgia caught Serena's gaze from across the arena, it was as if the sun had gone behind a cloud. Serena shot her a look of such hatred that Georgia shivered. Jodie and Lily were completely oblivious, riding in a little bubble of happiness, but Georgia had a very bad feeling in her stomach…

✩ ✩ ✩

"Georgia, wow, she's amazing, brilliant!" Jodie was bubbling with excitement as she untacked the palomino outside her stable. For a minute as Jackson hung his handsome black head over the stable door, watching his young mistress with interest, a look of sadness crossed Jodie's face. She reached over to give him a pat. "Although I wish I was still riding you."

"I know how you feel." Georgia understood completely. She would feel the same way if it was the other way round. "But Richard saw Jackson in action during the week, and his competition record speaks for itself," she reasoned. "It's your riding they're judging. If you get the place then you'll ride Jackson going forward."

Jodie smiled. "I know. Thanks again, Georgia."

The two girls were silent for a minute while Jodie stroked Jackson's nose thoughtfully, then she brightened. "Oh, I forgot to tell you something," she grinned. "Mum says I can stay here tonight, because it's the last night and everything. Which means that we can make sure Lily looks her best for tomorrow!"

"Great!" Georgia was over the moon. With only Serena and Sebastian around for company, it would be good to have a friend about the place. From the way Serena had looked at her earlier, Georgia wanted to stay as far away from her as possible!

✿ ✿ ✿

Once Melanie and Sophie had left Rosefolly, the rest of the evening passed happily. The only niggle for Georgia was how Melanie was really feeling. Ultimately, Lily was owned by Melanie. Uneasily Georgia wondered again if the owner of Redgrove was more disappointed than she was letting on.

Georgia was grateful to have Jodie with her as she joined Serena, Sebastian and Daisy for the last team meal before the assessment day. Together the two girls had given Lily a bath in the plush washroom on the main yard, helped by Amanda, who was thrilled Jodie was getting the chance to ride.

"It's better than a spa!" Georgia had exclaimed in amazement as she had examined the hot-water shower, the solarium light to dry the horses off and the massage devices for tired pony backs.

Lily had revelled in the luxury, used to the yard hose at Redgrove, which Georgia only ever used in the summer if it was warm enough. Now, basking in the heat from the lamps, Lily's golden coat shone and her mane dried into strands of fine silk. It wasn't a showing class tomorrow but Georgia loved to turn Lily out to the best of her ability.

Now, with Lily tucked up in her stable, munching on a hay net and wearing a clean woollen rug, Georgia wanted to spend a few minutes with the palomino before supper. Quietly, she stood with her arms round her neck, hoping her positive thoughts somehow got through to Lily. "Someone really depends on you tomorrow, sweetheart," she whispered. "Just try your best, for me."

CHAPTER FOURTEEN

The supper turned out to be a lot of fun, with both Daisy and Sebastian in high spirits. Serena was the only cloud on the horizon. Barely talking to Sebastian, and replying in monosyllabic answers when anyone tried to include her in the conversation, she was clearly still furious about Jodie riding Lily. As the evening wore on, Georgia felt her fears grow. She still thought Serena had put

134

the flint in Jackson's stable. Would she try to harm Lily to improve her chances? Georgia felt herself shiver as Serena stalked away from the table. She felt as though she didn't want to let Lily out of her sight, just in case her suspicions were confirmed.

Jodie listened quietly as Georgia whispered her idea to guard Lily that evening on the way out to the dorm rooms. "You might think I'm crazy." Georgia pushed the hair back from her face. "But I'm not leaving Lily's side tonight."

"OK," Jodie said slowly, pondering what Georgia was proposing. "But if you're camping out with Lily then so am I!"

Georgia smiled gratefully at her new friend, glad that she understood. She had spent a few evenings in the stables with Lily – the first night that she had arrived in Redgrove, then the night that Lily's foal Secret had been born, and finally on Christmas Eve when Lily had kept watch over Dan's orphan lambs. Georgia wasn't taking any chances where Lily was concerned. The little palomino was too precious!

✩ ✩ ✩

After the evening meal had been tidied away, the students were free to come and go as they pleased, as long as they stayed within the estate and were not on the yard after nine p.m. Georgia normally gave Lily some extra grooming or went up to her little dorm room and read. Most of the time she had been so tired after the intensive lessons that she was crashed out on her bed before the yard curfew. She always called or texted Dan in the free time after supper but, frowning, decided not to this time. She was going home tomorrow anyway. That didn't mean he couldn't contact her, and for a minute she smiled as she read a good-luck text from him. He didn't know yet that she wasn't riding, but it showed he still cared. Sighing, she put her phone back into her pocket. She had enough to think about for now.

Wrapped in pony rugs and sharing a bag of crisps, Georgia and Jodie sat opposite the pony boxes, watching Jackson and Lily as they dozed in the stables. Jodie knew the last check on the yard was done by the staff at ten o'clock, and so once this had been done the two girls had crept out of their dorm room, dressed in their warmest clothes. Georgia had a pair of tracksuit bottoms over her thermal leggings and a bobble hat on top of her blonde curls, whereas Jodie was wearing an all-in-one spotty fleece suit.

"Don't laugh," she'd grinned as Georgia had giggled at the sight of her onesie. "It was the warmest thing I could find!"

It was now half past midnight and the air was still, apart from the odd snort from the stables and the sound of munching on hay nets. "Does your

137

mum know you're here?" Georgia whispered to Jodie, who was half dozing, the hood of her onesie pulled up over her dark hair.

Jodie shook her head. "No," she murmured, "and we probably shouldn't tell her. I don't want to risk any trouble, not until I know her job is completely safe."

The girls were silent for a while. "What was he like? Your mum's horse?" Georgia asked, hoping it wasn't a sensitive subject.

Jodie gave a small, sad smile. "The best," she said quietly. "Mum could have gone right to the top on him."

"Do you know where he ended up?" Georgia asked curiously, and Jodie shrugged sadly. "He could be anywhere by now."

Georgia thought about this. There was just one thing she had been pondering while lying awake the previous night, and she had to ask Jodie. "If it hadn't been for what happened to your mum," she ventured carefully, "would you still want the squad place as badly?"

Jodie nodded her head vigorously, her dark hair rippling under the hood. "One hundred per cent," she said firmly. "I want to succeed."

Satisfied with this answer, Georgia smiled, and the two girls sat quietly as the minutes ticked by. Wondering if she had been totally wrong about Serena, Georgia was half considering calling it a night and going back to the warmth of her dorm bed, when through the gloom she noticed Lily's ears prick up. Georgia stood upright, her eyes searching in the dark. Nudging Jodie awake, she placed a finger to her lips. Startled, Jodie rubbed her eyes, just as Jackson raised his head and gave a small whicker. Straining to hear, Georgia felt her blood run cold as she heard an unmistakable cry for help…

CHAPTER FIFTEEN

Both girls were down from the hay bales in a flash. The noise was coming from the second pony block, where Serena and Sebastian's ponies were stabled. Running down the aisle, their footsteps ringing around the silent barn, Georgia and Jodie rounded the corner, raced across the courtyard and, to Georgia's horror, quickly discovered the noise was coming from Serena's pony's stable. Serena was crying in panic. The stable door was open, and in a couple of seconds Georgia took in the scene before her. Serena's big chestnut pony, Reggie, was cast, his body stuck against the stone wall of the stable. He couldn't get to his feet and he'd obviously been thrashing around as his neck was sweaty and his nostrils flared, but he was now lying quietly, as if waiting for help.

Georgia knew from Pony Club stable-management lessons that cast horses could present a huge risk to the people trying to help them, as well as to themselves. "Serena," she said trying to reason with her, "I need to go and get help from one of the grooms."

"No!" Serena rasped. "We'll get into massive trouble for being out here in the middle of the night. Please just help me get him upright."

Georgia thought quickly. She knew she ought to go and find one of the staff members who lived on site, but then she would need to explain what they were all doing on the yard at one in the morning. She thought about how Jodie was still worrying over her mum's job. She knew what she and Jodie were doing, but why was Serena down here?

Still, there wasn't time to think about that now. Serena's horse needed help. At least the big chestnut was calm, which gave Georgia a moment or two to gather her thoughts.

"Help him!" Serena wailed pitifully. "He's worth thousands!"

"Oh, shut up!" Georgia turned on her furiously. "It doesn't matter what he's worth. He's in distress and we need to get him up. Didn't you ever learn stable management?"

Serena glared sulkily at her, which answered that question.

"Lunge lines," Jodie piped up from Georgia's other side.

the PALOMINO PONY

Both girls turned to look at her. "I've seen it happen on yards that Mum's worked on," she continued. "We need to attach them to his legs and try to roll him back from the wall. Then he can get himself up."

"OK." Georgia tried to remain calm. It sounded simple when Jodie put it like that. She had never seen a cast horse, but it had been covered a few times in her Pony Club rallies. There were bound to be some lunge ropes hanging up in the storage area. Sprinting across from the stables, Georgia used her mobile-phone light to locate a couple of coiled-up lunge lines. She pulled them down and flew back to the chestnut's stable. Serena was still pacing around, but Jodie had crept inside to sit by the pony's head, keeping a safe distance from his legs and talking softly to him. Georgia started to uncoil the heavy lunge ropes.

"What now?" Serena asked shortly. "Are you

143

going to get him up?"

Ignoring Serena as best she could, Georgia weighed up the task ahead.

Jodie took charge. "OK. Georgia, can you put the rope over his front leg, the one nearest the wall? I'll keep him calm. Serena, can you do the same on his back legs?"

Quickly, Georgia looped the lunge line round Reggie's elegant fetlock. "Done!" she said breathlessly. "What about you, Serena?"

Standing back up, she saw Serena still in the same position, as if frozen, the rope still looped over her arm. "I . . . I can't," she whispered.

"Oh, for goodness' sake!" Georgia couldn't keep the frustration out of her voice. Time was ticking and they needed to move fast. Taking the lunge rope from Serena's hands, she moved forward to place it round the other foot when Reggie, finding a new burst of energy, made a fresh attempt to

scrabble to his feet.

"Georgia!" Jodie's warning cry was a fraction of a second too late.

Just as Georgia reached forward to secure the ropes round Reggie's fetlock, he kicked backwards, catching Georgia smartly on her thigh. For a minute she couldn't feel anything at all, and then she was aware of a searing, burning sensation in her leg, which took her breath away and brought tears to her eyes.

Reggie, sensing he was about to get help, stopped struggling and lay quietly once again, all the fight draining out of him. They had the ropes attached now. They just needed to get him up while they had the chance.

Gritting her teeth and biting down on her lip so she didn't cry, Georgia retreated backwards, safely out of Reggie's way. She thought she might pass out with the pain, and was just wondering how they were going to manage when she heard a familiar voice.

"What's going on?"

A tall figure appeared in the doorway in his pyjama bottoms, wellingtons and a hooded top. Sebastian!

"Serena?" he continued, looking around questioningly. "What are you doing out here so late?"

Serena mumbled a reply about making one last check on her horse, not looking at Sebastian.

"Rubbish!" Georgia hissed, adrenalin taking over from the incredible pain in her leg. "You were up to something, I just know you were!"

But there was no time to lose. Turning to Sebastian, Georgia handed him the lunge line. "Please help us," she said to him, and he nodded, quickly realising what was going on.

With Jodie still at Reggie's head keeping him

146

---

calm, and Georgia and Sebastian gently tugging at the lunge lines, Reggie gave a heave and began to push himself upward. A moment later he was back on his feet.

Realising Georgia was hurt, Sebastian moved in and released the ropes from Reggie's legs, as Jodie checked the pony for cuts or scrapes. Feeling sick and clutching her leg, Georgia slumped against the stable wall. Remarkably calm, Reggie had a good shake and then turned back to his hay net, seemingly completely unconcerned by what had happened.

"Well, he seems fine." Sebastian gave the big chestnut a pat and looked appraisingly at Georgia and Jodie. "It could have been a whole lot worse if you hadn't been here and got him up."

"Thanks, I guess," Serena said sulkily, barely looking at Georgia or Jodie. As she thrust her hands in her pocket, something fell out and landed on the

147

bedding. Sebastian bent down to pick it up.

"Serena…" Sebastian sounded serious. "What *is* this?" He held out a white plastic syringe, similar to those used to administer wormers. Time seemed to stand still.

"Give me that!" Serena hissed furiously, making a grab for it, and Sebastian held it a little higher, just out of her reach.

"Horse calmer, extra-strength," Sebastian continued as he read the packaging, his voice icy. "What exactly were you going to do with this?"

"It's nothing… I wasn't going to do anything!" Serena was scarlet with fury now, her eyes flashing dangerously.

"It doesn't look that way." Sebastian moved forward, a serious look on his face. "Serena, tell us what's going on."

Georgia stepped forward, feeling rage building within her. "Were you on your way to give it to

Lily?" she hissed.

Serena was totally backed into a corner as all three teenagers turned to look at her.

"All right!" Serena cried, putting her hands over her eyes. "Yes, I was. It wasn't going to hurt her. It's just what Dad uses to load the difficult ones. It would have worn off by the morning anyway. It was a stupid idea…" her voice trailed off.

"So, just to make Lily perform badly tomorrow then?" Georgia said slowly, realising what Serena's intentions had been.

"Look, you don't understand," Serena hissed, but it was as though the wind had been taken from her sails. "You don't know what it's like having a famous dad, with all that expectation on you!"

"Serena," Jodie said sadly, "what *happened* to you? We used to be friends."

"And then you came along and rode Jackson better than I ever could," Serena said, but she had slumped against the stable wall now, defeated.

"Serena, this isn't the way." Sebastian shook his head as he spoke. "I should have known something was up from the way Henry has been. He's working for your dad, isn't he?"

Serena nodded. All the fight had gone out of her now. "Henry advises dad on his German warmblood sales," she mumbled. "Dad paid him extra to get me a place and it was working, until Daisy rumbled him." She shot an angry look at Georgia. "If you hadn't got involved," Serena continued, "I wouldn't have done what I did; it was all under control."

"So the flint." Jodie pressed her fingers to her forehead. "That wasn't an accident?"

Serena shook her head.

150

"I knew it!" Georgia cried out.

"It's only a bruised sole," Serena cried as she tried to justify herself. "Nothing serious."

"But it nearly cost me my chance!" Jodie cried. "Serena, this *is* serious, you know that!"

"You can't prove anything." Serena was almost completely white now, her lips drained of colour as she shook her head furiously. Turning on her heel she fled back to her dorm room, leaving Sebastian, Jodie and Georgia completely speechless as Reggie gazed impassively after his young mistress.

CHAPTER SIXTEEN

Groggily, Georgia rolled over as the light crept under her dorm-room curtains, wincing as she stretched her leg. Pulling down her tartan pyjama bottoms she inspected the kick, which was rapidly forming a perfect horseshoe shape on her outer thigh. If it hadn't been for the bruise she might have believed the events of the previous night were just a bizarre dream. After Serena had run away there didn't seem to be anything to do but go back to bed, as Reggie was clearly fine.

Hobbling to her feet, Georgia limped over to the sink and splashed her face with cold water, examining her reflection in the small mirror. Her hair resembled something close to a bird's nest, but that was nothing new. She dressed as quickly as she could with her sore leg, thinking about what had happened. Serena's revelations during the night had made her even more determined that Jodie should win her place. She knew Serena had clouded her judgement about the whole week, but she was even more thankful she had given up the ride today. She just wanted to return to Redgrove.

☆ ☆ ☆

"All OK, Georgia?" Daisy raised an eyebrow as Georgia hobbled back to her place at the breakfast table, carrying her tray.

"Yes, fine!" Georgia tried to sound as bright

as possible. She knew that what Serena had said was true – there was no way they could prove that Serena had set out to sabotage Lily. And they would all be in deep trouble if they were found to have been in the stable yard in the middle of the night. There was no sign of Serena at the breakfast table, but Sebastian looked up and smiled when he saw Georgia, gesturing for her to take a seat opposite him.

Jodie, who had joined Georgia in the breakfast queue, sat down and gave Sebastian a shy smile. "I meant to ask you," she whispered, so no one could hear them. "What were you doing down in the yard last night?"

Sebastian gave a rueful smile. "I guessed Serena might be up to something after the way she was acting when she realised you were going to be riding Lily. I just didn't quite believe that Jackson's lameness was accidental, you know?"

154

Jodie nodded.

"I can't believe someone would go to those lengths!" Sebastian continued, shaking his head so that his floppy dark curls bounced up and down. "And I thought she was a friend!" He put down his knife and fork. "So I guess it's just you and me riding today." He gave Jodie a wide smile, his voice warm. "May the best rider win!"

✿ ✿ ✿

"Georgia, are you going to be OK?" Jodie's voice was full of concern as the two girls prepared Lily for the assessment day. Despite all the drama in the next-door stable block the previous night, Lily was as calm as ever, and as Georgia slipped on her bridle the little palomino nudged her hand, as if to reassure her she was going to try her best.

"Fine…" Georgia gritted her teeth, trying to ignore the pain. "Come on, she's as ready as she'll ever be." She felt a shiver run down her spine as she realised how close Serena had been to giving the calmer to Lily, her sweet, trusting little mare.

Expecting only Sebastian and Jodie to ride, Georgia gave a start of surprise as Serena clattered into the arena on Reggie. "Poor boy!" she exclaimed out loud, before she could stop herself. He must have been shaken up after his ordeal in the night and yet Serena was still determined to ride him. Most decent horsey people would have given the pony a day off to recover. Serena was clearly still desperate to prove herself, and with Henry Winters back at Rosefolly and on the panel, what would that mean for Jodie and Lily?

"What was that?" Daisy turned to Georgia in surprise.

"Oh, nothing," Georgia mumbled.

Georgia grimaced. Her leg was aching, and she knew it was getting worse. But she couldn't think about that now. *Come on, Lily,* she silently willed the palomino, who stood a good hand smaller than both Sebastian's and Serena's ponies, but had a lion-size heart.

Each candidate was to ride the dressage test that they had been practising during the week. It was a huge ask for Lily, who was only really used to Georgia's way of riding. But Jodie was a sensitive enough rider to realise that Lily only needed small aids in order to perform. Jodie had clearly noticed Lily's style during the past few days, and knew that the palomino preferred it when Georgia sat as quietly and as still as possible. They were warming up beautifully and Georgia gave her friend a big thumbs-up from the side of the school as her little mare trotted past. Jodie smiled and visibly relaxed.

The panel judges were in a little huddle at the far end of the school, but they were still watching and observing the warm-up. Sebastian was up first. His lovely bay pony was relaxed, and settled into an easy swinging stride. Sebastian was an amazing rider. His long legs hung down below his pony's tummy but in no way detracted from the overall picture. He rode a brilliant test and Georgia gave a little clap as he finished. She had seen a different side to Sebastian after last night's events. She wondered why Serena hadn't tried to get him knocked out of the assessment. Or maybe he had been her next target, after she'd finished with Jodie!

There was a short pause before Serena's assessment while the panel judges murmured among themselves. There were three in total who had a say, and each had to mark the riders individually. Henry Winters was as unsmiling as ever, but Richard, the judge who had come to watch the lessons earlier in the week, gave the students a kindly, encouraging smile. Serena started to trot Reggie round the outside of the arena. The chestnut gave a snort of frustration as she dug her outside heel into his side, so that it went unnoticed by the panel.

Poor Reggie. Georgia shook his head. She hoped that whatever the outcome of the day, he would be looked after, and not just sold on if he didn't live up to expectation.

Reggie's kind nature shone through during his assessment. Despite his dramatic evening and Serena's harsh hands, it was clear he was trying his very best. But Serena's riding fell short of Sebastian's and Jodie's. Richard and the other panel judge gave Serena a polite smile. Richard tilted his hat at her, while Henry looked stonily ahead. Georgia wondered if he was still being bribed to try to get Serena a squad place. Surely he could see both Sebastian and Jodie were more deserving?

Now it was Lily's turn. As Georgia watched

the golden mare trot round the outside of the arena, Jodie sitting quietly in the saddle with her long dark ponytail bouncing up and down, she felt a huge mix of emotions. Pride, knowing how much she had achieved with the little mare, though a smidgen of sadness and regret. But – despite it all – Georgia knew she'd made the right decision. She just hoped Melanie would be able to understand!

CHAPTER SEVENTEEN

As Lily trotted beautifully up the centre line, Georgia sat down as gingerly as possible on the benches, trying to take the weight off her leg, rubbing it gently. She noticed Daisy give her a sideways frown before settling down to watch Lily's performance. But Daisy was soon distracted enough not to look across to Georgia and question her further.

At every turn, every extension, every transition, Georgia found herself riding alongside Jodie. She knew exactly what each move would feel like, and watched with growing pleasure as Lily performed a foot-perfect test. Georgia almost forgot about her injury as she clapped as hard as she could, tears springing to her eyes. Lily had given Jodie the best possible chance of a place, and she couldn't do more than that.

"Thank you, thank you, thank you!" Jodie was completely overwhelmed as she untacked the little palomino back in her stable. Georgia had limped back to join them as quickly as possible. The pain in her leg was making her feel a little nauseous and she had paled even further under her freckles. Luckily Daisy was too wrapped up in a conversation with Sebastian to notice, but Jodie could clearly tell Georgia was in pain.

"Do you think we should go to hospital?" she

whispered, her voice concerned, but Georgia shook her head firmly.

"It's just a bruise," she muttered unconvincingly. She was determined to hear the outcome of the assessment day.

Before Jodie could say any more she was swept aside by her mum, who was full of congratulations for her daughter.

Georgia leaned heavily against Lily's side as the little mare snuffled her in concern. She was still standing in the stable, trying not to cry, when Richard, one of the panel judges, cleared his throat as he leaned over the stable door, making her jump.

"Hello, young lady," he said in a kind voice, removing his trilby hat.

"Hello," Georgia said politely in reply, looking around her, feeling a little unsure. She hadn't ridden, so what was he doing here?

"I've come to talk to you about your mare," Richard explained. "I know you gave up your chance to go for a squad place, and that's fine, your choice. But it's actually your pony I'm more interested in."

Georgia took a deep breath as Richard explained that someone had spotted Lily and wanted to purchase her for an up-and-coming junior dressage rider, who was aiming for the national team. They had put in an offer of many thousands of pounds. He wanted to know if Georgia was interested in such an offer.

"I'm afraid that she doesn't officially belong to me," Georgia mumbled, her head spinning. "It's not my decision."

"I'm aware of that. I've already been in contact with Mrs Hayden," the judge said.

Georgia felt the room starting to spin more quickly. She couldn't blame Mel for considering

164

other options for the little mare, as Georgia had decided not to compete. The air was muffled and heavy, and suddenly Richard's voice sounded very slow and very far away. As Georgia's knees buckled, the last thing she was aware of was Lily's start of surprise, and then the stable went black.

"Georgia, Georgia?"

Groggily, Georgia opened her eyes. It took her a minute or two to realise where she was – sitting outside Lily's stable. Jodie was crouching next to her, holding a plastic tumbler full of water while a kindly-looking paramedic was on her other side. Daisy was on the phone and seemed to be calling Georgia's mum.

Georgia pulled herself up gingerly, wincing as she remembered the bruise on her leg. "What happened?" She felt as though she had been asleep for days.

"You fainted!" Jodie exclaimed. "Richard raised the alarm. Luckily an ambulance was in the area and so they were here very quickly."

"Have you hurt yourself on that leg?" the paramedic asked gently, and Georgia nodded. She slowly rolled down her jeans and revealed a perfect horseshoe-shaped bruise, now a dramatic purple.

The paramedic whistled. "Now, that's a bruise!" he said. "We'll need to take you in to get that checked out."

Daisy, snapping the phone shut, turned in alarm and gave a start as she noticed Georgia's leg. She gasped. "What on earth happened?"

"It's my fault," Georgia mumbled as Daisy inspected her leg more closely.

"Let's get you to hospital," Daisy said grimly. "You can explain everything to me there."

CHAPTER EIGHTEEN

The hospital was located in the small market town about five minutes away from Rosefolly Equestrian Centre. Georgia and Daisy had travelled there in the ambulance together. The doctors had checked her over and her leg was OK, just very bruised. Georgia needed to rest with her leg up for a few days to allow the bruising to heal.

She was lost in thought as she tried to make

herself comfortable in the hard bed. Everything that she had decided – to take Lily back to Redgrove – felt as though it was slipping away. She knew that Melanie would have to seriously consider the offer for Lily.

"So, are you going to tell me what's been going on now?" Daisy asked from her seat next to Georgia's bed.

"It was my fault," Georgia repeated. She may as well tell Daisy the truth. "It was my idea to go down to the yard and guard Lily."

"Guard Lily? What do you mean?"

Daisy listened quietly as Georgia explained how she had wanted to keep watch over Lily's stable during the night because she had been worried about sabotage, and how she had persuaded Jodie to join her. They had been guarding her stable when they heard Reggie in trouble.

"And that's how you were kicked?" Daisy

frowned, and Georgia nodded.

"Sebastian found the syringe of calmer that Serena was going to use on Lily, but we can't prove anything."

"So that's why you didn't say anything?" Daisy asked gently. "You thought you and Jodie would be in trouble for breaking yard rules."

Georgia nodded again, hanging her head. "It's just that getting a squad place meant everything to Jodie. I didn't want her to get in trouble."

Daisy was silent, digesting what Georgia had told her. Then she smiled. "Jodie won't be in trouble and neither will you. I'm going to make sure of it." She sat down on the end of Georgia's bed. "I believe you about Serena. I think she was responsible for Jackson's lameness." Daisy patted Georgia's hand as she continued. "I think Jodie has got something she wants to tell you." She gestured at the door for Jodie to come in.

Jodie walked in. She was with her mum, who must have driven her to the hospital. Jodie was beaming from ear to ear as she flopped down next to Daisy, still wearing her riding gear.

"We did it, Georgia! I got the place and it's all thanks to you!" she cried, reaching over to hug her friend.

"Ouch!" Georgia said, smiling, as she rearranged her leg, and Jodie gasped.

"Oh, my goodness, Georgia. I'm so sorry, I forgot about that!"

"It's OK," Georgia said truthfully. In fact, her bruised leg was already feeling better after some painkillers, and Jodie's news had filled her with happiness. Lily, her little mare, had given Jodie back her dream! She just felt a little sad that she had missed the announcement. "That's brilliant news! But how did Serena take it?" she asked cautiously.

170

"You missed all the drama!" Jodie was waving her hands around as she explained how Richard and Henry had had a huge argument before Henry had stormed off. Henry had given Jodie and Sebastian the lowest marks he could get away with, and Serena the highest. This had raised eyebrows among the panel, especially as it meant that Serena had come out on top, with Henry's marks dragging down Jodie and Sebastian. Richard had then been handed a letter outlining Henry's involvement with the Van der Hawks' yard.

"Who gave him that?" Georgia asked in astonishment, and a frown crossed Daisy's face.

"It was me," she said. "I've been doing a bit of investigative work over the last couple of days." Daisy explained she had raised enough suspicions among the panel to confront Henry, who wasn't able to deny it. His scores had been written off and the allegations would be looked into by the officials. "We can't prove that Serena set out to harm Jackson and Lily, of course," Daisy said. "So we just have to hope that she's learned her lesson, and that she now knows that she can't have everything her way."

Georgia nodded as she sank back down on to the hospital pillow. She was utterly delighted that Jodie had her place. But Richard's words regarding the offer for Lily were playing over and over in her mind.

Georgia felt as though her stomach was turning over in knots. Although the doctor had told her that she had fainted because she had been standing on her bad leg all day, Georgia knew it had to be more than that. It had to be the possibility of Lily being sold. The thought of losing Lily was enough to break her heart in two.

CHAPTER NINETEEN

Given a clean bill of health, Georgia was soon discharged from the hospital with strict instructions to ice and rest her leg, and take some more painkillers. Daisy drove her back the short distance to Rosefolly and as they wound up the long drive through the beautiful grounds, Georgia reflected on how much had happened during the week since Melanie had driven the horsebox up.

She had realised what it was that made her happiest, but in doing so had put Lily firmly in front of the people who could make big things happen for her. As they rounded the corner and she saw the Haydens' familiar dark-green lorry, she felt her heart sink. Melanie was deep in conversation with the judges on the panel. Even worse, she was holding what looked like an envelope, and nodding intently. Suddenly Georgia was dreading the journey home.

"Georgia!" Melanie was all smiles as she climbed gingerly out of Daisy's car. "I was so worried. Your poor mum rang me while I was on my way here!"

"I'm OK." Georgia limped across to where they were standing outside Lily's stable. Truthfully, the pain in her leg was nothing in comparison to the pain she would feel if Lily was sold.

"Gave me a bit of a fright, young lady," Richard chuckled as he patted Lily, who was staring at

174

Georgia with her ears pricked.

Georgia smiled weakly and tears stung her eyes as Richard shook Mel's hand.

"Just let me know your decision," he said, tilting his hat at both of them.

"Thanks, Richard. Ready to go home?" Melanie patted Georgia's shoulder, and she nodded. She'd never been more ready to get back to Redgrove.

☆ ☆ ☆

While Melanie packed up Lily's belongings, telling Georgia firmly to sit on a hay bale and rest, Georgia gave her new friend Jodie a big hug. She decided their friendship was one of the best things to come out of her week at the stables.

Sebastian, loading his big bay into the most luxurious metallic-white horsebox, gave her a grin and high-fived her. He had turned out to be not so bad after all, and Georgia was amused to witness him swap phone numbers with a blushing

Jodie. It made her think of Dan, and she frowned. She wondered yet again what Dan had been up to during the week when everyone was telling her a different story. Was she about to lose both her beloved mare *and* Dan? Or were neither of them ever really hers to lose?

After saying goodbye to Daisy, Georgia clambered into the front of the lorry and waved through the window. Melanie expertly guided the horsebox out of the yard and down the long drive, as Georgia gazed at the deer that were grazing next to the road. She longed to ask Melanie about Richard's offer but didn't dare raise the subject as she dreaded what the answer might be. They chatted lightly about the week, and Sophie's cross-country ride on Wilson, but it was obvious that there were unspoken words hanging between them.

Melanie seemed about to tell her something, but

kept stopping herself. "I'm going to make a stop in a few minutes," she told Georgia after about half an hour had passed. "I could do with a coffee and I'm sure Lily would appreciate being looked in on."

"OK." Georgia paused. Then, before she could stop herself, her words came out all in a rush. "So the team selector has made an offer for Lily," she mumbled. "They want her for the young riders' team, don't they? I just wondered... I mean ... would you sell her?"

"Well..." Melanie kept her eyes firmly on the road as she replied, and Georgia felt her heart crash through her chest. This couldn't be happening.

"You know that's the sort of offer an owner really should consider, Georgia ... and Lily really is a brilliant pony." Melanie spoke as gently as possible, as if trying to lessen Georgia's hurt.

Georgia felt her throat constrict and her legs

grow shaky. She tried to stop the tears from spilling over as she nodded, feeling totally numb.

Flicking the indicator, Melanie eased the big green lorry off the motorway and came to a steady halt in the service-station car park. Georgia felt Lily shift her weight in the back of the vehicle.

"We'll talk about this more in a minute. I'll go and get the drinks; you check Lily," Melanie said as she unbuckled her seat belt and reached for her purse, which was sitting under the dashboard. Opening it, she scrabbled around and then gave a frown. "Oh, Georgia," she said. "You don't have a spare pound, do you? I haven't got any change."

Georgia nodded and reached into her backpack. Pulling out a one-pound coin she handed it over to Melanie, who smiled.

"Thanks!" she called as she jumped down from the lorry. "I won't be long." Taking the opportunity to have a few precious minutes with the little

178

palomino, Georgia clambered into the living area and opened the jockey door. Lily blinked back at her before giving a whicker. She was happily munching at her hay net, and she paused as Georgia rested her face against her cheek, feeling the mare so warm and solid, before closing her eyes and giving a shuddering sigh. Lily was the best thing that had ever happened to her.

But Georgia knew Lily's future was out of her hands. Melanie legally owned the little palomino pony, and there was nothing Georgia could do about that.

CHAPTER TWENTY

"Hot chocolate, your favourite!" Melanie called at the entrance to the living area, and reluctantly Georgia gave Lily a final pat before going back to her seat. She and Melanie sat in silence, sipping the hot drinks. Finally Georgia plucked up the courage to ask Melanie what she was going to do.

"Georgia," Melanie said gently. "I've had to really think about this carefully."

As she spoke, Georgia felt her heart thumping and her palms grow hot. She thought she might start to cry, and swallowed hard as Melanie continued, talking about a once in a lifetime opportunity. Finally, she picked up an envelope from the seat next to Georgia, and handed it over. "The offer is in this envelope."

Reluctantly, slowly, Georgia tore the envelope open and unfolded the letter. The offer was for a huge amount. Her eyes swam with tears, before she gave a start, and looked closely at the letter as a smile crossed Melanie's face. The letter was addressed to Miss Georgia Black, not Mrs Melanie Hayden.

Looking from the letter to Mel and back again as Melanie tried to hide her grin, Georgia shook her head, trying to understand. "What?" Her voice was croaky as she tried to speak. "I don't get it! Why is the letter addressed to me? I'm not her owner!"

"It's *your* choice to make." Melanie patted Georgia's hand. "Georgia, Lily is yours! I may have officially owned her but she's always been *your* pony. I need to send her paperwork off to the Welsh Pony Society to transfer her ownership over to you, and the pound you gave me was just to make it all legal. It's an age-old horseman thing." She gave a wink. "I didn't mean to make you worry so much, but I wanted to get everything sorted out before I told you."

Georgia shook her head, feeling totally bewildered as Melanie explained she had been planning to sell Lily to Georgia all along but then Richard had made his offer and that had brought things to a head.

"Don't you recognise where we are?" Melanie smiled and gestured around her at the service station.

Georgia thought hard. It looked like every other one of the concrete-grey services they had driven into on one of their many journeys in the horsebox over the years.

"It's the one we stopped at on the way back from Wales – do you remember?" Melanie said gently. "You and Dan were soaking wet and freezing cold and Lily was looking a state, but you saw something beautiful in her. You were the one who convinced *me* to take a chance! She's been your special mare since then, a pony of a lifetime! And you made the right choice yesterday. You followed your heart."

Completely choked, Georgia shook her head again, trying to find the right words. She couldn't speak, and managed to only croak out *thank you*. It felt completely inadequate but Melanie understood. She turned the key in the ignition and gave Georgia a big smile.

"Come on," she chuckled. "Let's get you home to Redgrove, where you *both* belong."

☆ ☆ ☆

"Georgia, I've missed you so much!" Emma hugged her friend as Georgia climbed carefully down from the cab after the horsebox pulled into Redgrove. The lights were on in the yard and Wilson, Callie and Santa whinnied in unison, ears pricked as Lily answered them.

"I've missed you as well." Georgia linked her arm in Emma's. "It's been quite a week." Looking around the yard, she felt herself relax. It was early evening and the ponies were in for the night. The yard had never looked so welcoming. Lily was soon settled back into her stable with a sigh, as Emma and Melanie helped remove her travelling bandages and put her stable rug on.

"Where's Will?" Georgia asked as she leaned against the stable door for support. Her leg was stiff after the long journey and she was looking forward to a hot bath when she got home.

"Here!" a familiar voice replied and, turning, Georgia grinned at the sight of the ever-cheerful Will, who was just returning from the hay barn. "Hey, G!" he chuckled, sweeping her up into a hug. "I heard a bit about what happened. For the record, I think you made the right choice." He paused. "If you don't want to do something one hundred per cent, then it's not for you."

"So you don't think Lily is wasted then?" Georgia asked, still looking for reassurance, and Will shook his head.

"No way," he said firmly. "She's proved herself already for you. Also, with the way you turned her around, people will be queuing up to send their ponies to you, if that's what you still want to do when you leave school."

Georgia smiled. Will was really sensible when it

came to horsey matters, partly because of his own experience. "By the way," she asked curiously, realising Dan wasn't there to meet her, "have you been hanging around with Dan loads this week?" Her heart sank as she noticed Will couldn't quite meet her eye.

"Well, a bit, here and there, haven't seen that much of him..." he mumbled vaguely, and Georgia knew she'd been right – Dan *was* hiding something. That was probably why he wasn't here tonight, she thought sadly. She had wanted him to be the first person she told about Lily officially belonging to her.

Feeling suddenly exhausted after such an intense week, she had never been more grateful to see her mum's little car trundle slowly up the drive and Mrs Black jump out to give Georgia a huge hug. "I've missed you both!" Georgia's mum reached out a hand to Lily, who stuck her head over the stable door, knowing Mrs Black normally came with carrots for a treat!

"Did you know, Mum, about Lily?" Georgia reached an arm round the little mare's neck. It still hadn't sunk in yet that she owned her, and Mrs Black laughed.

"We've been planning it a while," she said with a wink. "We will come to some arrangement over the livery, but Mel said you can work in your holidays towards it. But as long as your schoolwork doesn't slip, I'm happy for you. I've seen a real change in you, Georgia, since Lily came along." Then, noticing her daughter wince as she shifted the weight on her legs, she took Georgia's arm. "Come on, you," she said firmly. "I think you've had enough for one day."

Chapter Twenty-One

Rolling over in her bed, Georgia blinked at the light streaming through her curtains. Pip, overjoyed her young mistress was home again, crawled on her tummy up towards her, covering her face in kisses.

Chuckling, Georgia patted her. "Sorry, old girl," she smiled. "I can't walk you up to the stables today. Come on, let's see if Mum will take us up."

Her mum was already up and nursing a coffee

at the kitchen table and was only too happy to give Georgia a lift. The bruising on Georgia's leg was turning into a rainbow of colour, but the swelling was going down and it felt much better. Even so, she couldn't manage her normal cycle ride. Dan had texted her when she arrived home the previous evening, promising her he would see her today, but she had been too exhausted to reply.

A crescendo of whinnies greeted Georgia as she limped through the yard gates that morning. With the sunshine burning off the last of the earlier frost and daffodils starting to appear in the neat flower beds bordering the little yard, Redgrove had never looked prettier. Even better, Lily, her very own pony, was waiting in the stable. Georgia smiled happily. It would take a while to get used to saying that she owned her beloved pony!

It took a couple of seconds to work out that there was a pony missing from the line-up. Wilson's kind bay face wasn't hanging over his stable door as usual, and Georgia felt her heart stop. However, Will appeared by her side and told her that Wilson was absolutely fine.

"Come and see him, G. He's in the outdoor arena!" Will took her arm and guided Georgia towards the small woodchipped school where she and Will practised their flatwork.

Bemused, Georgia followed him. Why were Will's eyes sparkling with mischief? As she rounded the hay barn, putting her hands over her eyes to shield against the bright sunshine, Georgia had to look twice. Mel was in the middle of the arena, holding on to a lunge line, and Wilson was trotting obediently round her in a circle. The figure riding the steady bay looked familiar. The rider was concentrating hard, was a little wobbly and holding firmly on to a neck strap, but they looked pretty good. It was Dan!

"What the..." Georgia rubbed her eyes again, unsure if she was seeing things as, smiling to herself, Mel brought Wilson to a halt.

Patting the big bay on his neck, Dan swung easily down from the saddle and, holding on to the reins, crossed over to Georgia and hugged her with his free hand.

"What's going on?" Georgia asked again, totally bewildered.

"This is what I've been doing all week!" Dan grinned, his arm still round Georgia, dropping a kiss on the top of her head. "I figured if you can't beat them, join them!"

Georgia listened, a slow smile spreading across her face as Dan explained that everyone had helped him – Will, Sophie, Mel and Emma. He had been having lessons every day so he could surprise Georgia. He had been practising every minute he wasn't at the farm, and Mel had even been giving him stable-management lessons. "Only no one thought to keep to the same story. We should have thought about that!" Dan chuckled, and Georgia nodded, feeling embarrassed; it was all making sense now!

"I was so worried!" she blurted out before she could stop herself. "I thought… I thought…" she stammered, trying to think of the right words.

"You thought I'd grown bored of you," Dan said gently, and he smiled his wide sunny smile. "No way, Georgia. Quite the opposite. This is what we can do in the summer when I'm not milking and stuff. You can teach me how to do that funny long trot you do!"

"Extensions!" Georgia laughed. "And that would be amazing," she added shyly. She couldn't believe Dan had been learning to ride in secret, just so he could spend more time with her. Life was full of surprises at the moment. Her tummy backflipped several times. And to think she had been worrying all week over nothing. The two of them smiled at each other, and Georgia blushed as she noticed Melanie wink at her. Never in a million years had she expected this, and yet it seemed so right.

✿ ✿ ✿

A few weeks later Dan and Georgia hacked together down the quiet lanes back towards Redgrove. It was a warm March day and the verges were covered in daffodils and primroses, a welcome splash of colour after such a cold winter. Both ponies were in high spirits. Dan was a natural in the saddle, as his easy affinity with animals meant he was relaxed and kind, and he had just had his first canter across the open downs above Redgrove. He was still grinning from ear to ear, declaring it the best adrenalin rush.

As they wandered back to the yard, in no particular hurry, Georgia reflected on how happy she was with her decision about not taking Lily on any further. They had a few shows lined up, but not many, and Janey, who had been good-natured about Georgia's withdrawal from the assessment day, had signed Lily up straight away for the Pony Club dressage team. Georgia was already practising hard for the area competition in a couple of weeks' time. She was in regular contact with Jodie, who had moved Jackson to Rosefolly now that she had a training bursary. Her first dressage competition as a squad member had been a huge success and she had taken the individual silver on Jackson.

Henry Winters had been fired from the yard once Rosefolly's owners had returned from their holiday in Australia. He was currently the subject of a major investigation that was now being reported in *Horse & Hound*, and his and Michael Van der Hawk's scheming was the talk of the shows. Georgia found herself feeling a little sorry for Serena, who had returned home to her family yard without her longed-for squad place. She had been totally awful but Georgia wondered what pressure she had been under to make her behave so badly. She was sure Serena would pop up some time in the future; she was just that sort of girl.

Still, whatever happened, Georgia would always have Lily beside her. Laughing, Georgia reached forward and hugged the loyal golden mare. It still hadn't sunk in that Lily was hers, not even when the pony passport had been returned to her, stamped with Georgia's name. Georgia remembered what she had told Jodie back at the training camp. Being with Lily was her dream, and now it had come true. Melanie had been right. The palomino pony had always been hers, right from the very beginning. Always and forever.

ACKNOWLEDGEMENTS

Nosy Crow would like to thank Katy Marriott Payne for letting her lovely palomino pony star on the covers of this series.

Have you read all the wonderful
Palomino Pony books?

the
PALOMINO
✿PONY
COMES
HOME

the
PALOMINO
✿PONY
RIDES
OUT

the
PALOMINO
✿PONY
WINS
THROUGH

the
PALOMINO
✿PONY
RUNS
FREE

the
PALOMINO
✿PONY
ON PARADE

If you enjoyed this series, you'll love...

RED
MOON
RISING

PAULA HARRISON

DARK TREE SHINING

PAULA HARRISON